Witch Glitch

Book 2 , Magic and Mayhem

By

Robyn Peterman

Copyright © 2015 by Robyn Peterman

Cover by *Rebecca Poole, dreams2media*
Edited by *Meg Weglarz, megedits.com*

Acknowledgements

Thank you to so many. Writing may be solitary, but it takes a hell of a lot of people to help finalize the finished product!

Donna McDonald, I would be toast without you. You are my friend, Mystery Science Theatre partner and so much more.

Thank you. Rebecca Poole you are a cover guru and I don't want to do a book without you!

Meg Weglarz, your editing rocks!

My beta readers, Melissa, Donna, Susan and Wanda, you are the BOMB! My Pimpettes are my backbone and I am humbled by your support.

My family makes everything worth it and I adore you!

And my readers... I would be nothing without you.

Dedication

For Fat Bastard, Boba Fett and Jango Fett. You guys made my life happier. Forgive me for exaggerating your girth (except for Fat Bastard).

I miss you and hope your Next Adventure is as amazing as the time you spent with me.

Chapter 1

"What in the hell does that asswaffle think he's doing?" I snapped as I narrowed my eyes at the scene unfolding on the beautiful front lawn of my newly inherited house.

Crawling up onto the window seat I pressed my face against the glass to make sure I was seeing things correctly. Unfortunately, I was.

Chuck, the ginormous bear Shifter, had concocted a noose and was trying to hang himself in a large tree. This was not going to happen in my yard. Dead stuff smelled horrific and I had an over active gag reflex, as did most witches I knew.

Opening the widow with a pissed off blast of magic, I leaned out and prepared to zap his idiot ass. As the newly minted town Shifter Whisperer—or Shifter Wanker as I liked to refer to my job title—I wasn't about to heal a self-inflicted broken neck.

"Chuck, what in the Goddess's name do you think you're doing?" I shouted as he fell off the ladder he was standing on and plopped ungracefully to the ground with a thud.

"Well, I was trying to hang myself until you scared the bejesus out of me," he explained logically as if what he was doing was even remotely logical.

"Well okay, but you're going to have to take your freak show to someone else's tree. I have a lot of shit to do today and watching you die is not on my list."

"But I have to do it here," he informed me as he ambled up to the porch.

"I am about to ask a question I have no desire to know the

5

answer to—but *why?*"

Shifters were the weirdest species ever. I had always thought witches were nuts. We had nothing on the Shifters.

"I can't tell you," he mumbled into his shoulder.

He was a beautiful and kind man and I liked him, which annoyed me. I was getting far too attached to the oddballs in Assjacket, West Virginia. I had chosen to stay after I had paid my penance to the Witch Council, but if these dorks were going to pull stunts like hanging themselves in my trees, I was out of here.

"I call bullshit," I snapped. "You can't just off yourself in someone's Silver Oak and not tell them why. It's rude."

"I'm sorry, Zelda," he apologized as he rocked back and forth in embarrassment. "If I could tell you I would, but I can't break the rules. I could end up naked and wedged in a time warp with elevator music."

"You lost me," I said as I reconsidered zapping his ass just for making my brain work too hard at 8 AM.

"It's no big deal. I can try again another time when you're out shopping. I'll just be on my way," he said with a smile.

I really wanted to shut the window and pretend I hadn't just seen the dumbass try to end his life, but my newly found conscience wasn't on the same page.

Biting down hard on my tongue, I attempted to keep my words from flying out of my mouth—no fucking go. Apparently speak first and think later was my new motto. Damn it.

"Chuck, um…emotions and being nice are not really my thing, but I'm feeling kind of wonky here. Are you depressed? Can I heal that?" I asked as mentally slapped myself for caring.

"Actually, I'm not down at all," he replied with a shrug and a happy little grunt. "I'm quite content, but thank you for your concern."

"Ooookay then, you should probably take the ladder and rope with you," I mumbled not quite sure what was socially acceptable to say in a situation like this.

"Can I just leave them here for next time?"

"Um, no. You can't."

"Alrighty," he said as he gathered up his death tools and loaded them into his truck. "Oh and by the way, when I do bite it, I'd like you to have my truck."

"Really?" I squealed with excitement and then purposely banged my head against the windowsill. It was a kickass truck, but I'd rather win it in a poker game than inherit it due to his demise.

"Absolutely not," I hissed to cover my wildly inappropriate

reaction. "You are not going to die. I will kill you if you do."

"Would you?" he asked hopefully.

"Would I what?" I rolled my eyes in exasperation.

"Kill me?"

"Holy shitballs, I wasn't serious," I shouted. "I'm the freakin' Shifter Wanker. It's my job to heal you furry jackasses, not kill you."

"Right," he said with a nod and a grin. "My bad."

"I should say so," I muttered.

"Do you still need me to fix the refrigerator?" he asked.

"Um... yeah unless your going to lock yourself in it and freeze to death."

He chuckled and slapped his knee. "Nope, too big for that. I'll come back later today and fix it up like new."

"And you'll leave the death tools at home?" I asked warily.

"Will do," he said with a wave and drove away.

I closed the window and flopped down on the cushy couch. This day was going to be a long one. I could feel it in my bones.

"Zelda?" a loud masculine voice boomed from the kitchen. "Do you want French toast or pancakes?"

I heaved a put upon sigh and stood up. "French toast would be a nice change, Naked Dude. But where are all the groceries coming from? Are you using bad credit cards again?"

"I really wish you would just call me Dad," Naked Dude said as he stuck his head out from the kitchen. "I'm not naked you know."

He was correct. He wasn't naked. However, he *was* buck-ass naked when I made his acquaintance only a few weeks before. It had been traumatic and repulsive. No one should have to see their father's nads. Ever. Not to mention he'd been my cat for the past two years.

As the story goes, he never knew about me. When he found out he had a daughter he tried to contact me, but my not so motherly mother had put a spell on him that turned him into a mangy cat. That mangy cat had become my familiar, much to my disgust. The spell could only be broken if he gained my love.

Of course it took him almost dying for me to admit I loved him. Now we were trying to get to know each other. It was challenging and somewhat amazing, not that I would admit that to him. I'd always thought he didn't want me—at least that's what my mother had told me. The relief I felt when I learned he never knew about me was so absurd I ignored it. I wasn't real good at maintaining relationships, but I was going to try.

"Look, I could drop the Naked and just call you Dude.

Would that help?" I bargained.

His grin was infectious and his sparkling green eyes matched my own. "It's a start."

"I could call you Fabio. That *is* your name," I added as I sat down and dug in. I'd broach the bad credit card issue after my stomach was full.

"I'd really like you to try Dad," he said as he added two more pieces of French toast to my plate.

Thank the Goddess witches had crazy fast metabolism or I'd be the size of a house. Eating was my favorite hobby next to shopping and Naked Dude could cook.

"And I'd really like the Prada bag that isn't out yet," I shot back.

"Not a problem," Naked Dude slash Fabio slash Dad said with a sly grin on his ridiculously handsome face.

My dad, for lack of a better word, liked to buy slash steal me designer duds and accessories. This was a bad thing. I knew it was a bad thing. It was a terrible, bad, illegal thing. However, his logic that he also used his questionable credit cards to give tens of thousands to charity made me feel a little better about keeping my dubious booty.

"You can do that?" I asked as I poured an obscene amount of syrup on the mountain of French toast.

"I can transport to Milan, buy the bag and be back in an hour or two," he told me as he took the sugary goo from my hands before I could drain the bottle.

"*Buy* being the operative word."

"But of course," he replied with an innocent look that probably worked on most people except me.

"But I would have to call you Dad," I pondered aloud.

"That's the deal."

I considered it. I'm ashamed to say I really did.

"I'm not there yet, Naked Dude—I mean Dude. As much as it pains me to say no to the bag—and it does pain me, I'm just not ready to take that step."

"I understand," he said as he lovingly tucked some of my wild red locks that mirrored his behind my ear. "I'll just get the bag and keep it in my closet until you're ready."

"That's unacceptable, not to mention blackmail," I said as I slapped his hand away and tried to bite back my giggle. "You totally suck."

"I know." He gave me a lopsided grin and transported to Milan in a cloud of silver smoke.

"What a dick," I mumbled to no one since I was finally alone.

8

My year had been an interesting one. I'd spent nine months in the magic pokey for killing my cat who miraculously rose from the dead and turned out to be my father. To be fair to me, it had been an accident. When I heard the first crunch I'd freaked out so much that I hit reverse and drive simultaneously a few times before I got out of my car and screamed bloody murder. I buried him in a new Prada shoebox and left the super soft shoe bags inside as a blanket and a pillow. After Naked Dude's resurrection, he'd complimented me on his cozy coffin.

Of course, it didn't matter to Baba Yaga, the most powerful and horrendously dressed witch in existence, that it had been an accident or that my cat slash dad had actually lived. I had to serve time in the pokey with a heinous cellmate, Sassy the Violent Witch from Hell. Not that she enjoyed that moniker so much, but annoying her even a fraction as much as she had me helped pass the time.

After my release, I found out I had an aunt who had left me her house—a dead aunt I never knew. My mission ended up being avenging her, taking over her job as the Shifter Whisper and maintaining the magical balance in Assjacket, West Virginia. I had no clue what Sassy's mission had ended up being, I was just delighted to be rid of her.

It hurt like a motherfucker to heal the random wounds of all the idiot Shifters in town, but secretly I kind of liked my new job—not the pain—the job. I'd never stayed anywhere very long and had few friends to show for it. Sassy did not count. Belonging somewhere was new to me and it felt nice. However, I refused to get used to it. I was a survivor and had gone most of my life as a loner. Less messy that way.

The best thing about Assjacket was Mac. The redonkulously hot wolf Shifter who mistakenly thought I was his mate.

Speaking of hot asses, broad shoulders and outstanding lip locking, I had a lunch date with the werewolf this afternoon.

Maybe today wouldn't turn out as badly as it had begun.

Chapter 2

"How do I look?" I asked Naked Dude as I twirled around in my rockin' Alice and Olivia mini dress with my hot pink combat boots and cashmere shrug.

"Nice, I suppose," he replied cautiously.

Naked Dude was never one to hold back an opinion and his reticence pissed me off. He'd been back from Milan for an hour and it took everything I had not to ransack his closet for the Prada bag.

"Suppose?" I asked with narrowed eyes as green sparks began fly from my fingertips.

"It's not the outfit." He sighed dramatically and backed away from the impending fireworks. "It's the company you're keeping."

"I thought you approved of Mac."

"He's tolerable for a werewolf, but it would be wonderful if you'd meet a nice stable warlock and settle down, have a few witch babies and make me a grandwarlock," he explained as he handed me a fork and a bowl of raw cookie dough to snack on.

"This is exactly why I can't call you Dad," I informed him with a mouthful. "You're delusional. There is no such thing as a nice stable warlock. You are the most stable warlock I've ever met and you're certifiable."

"Thank you... I think."

"It wasn't a compliment, Na... Dudio. And let me just add that I am no prize."

"Of course you are," he interrupted. "You're beautiful, smart, powerful, compassionate, kind, and you're a wonderful eater."

"Have you been living here?" I shouted. "Sure I might be hot and powerful. Sure I can eat like a horse, but I am *not* kind or compassionate. I have never maintained any sort of relationship in my entire life. At least Mac still likes me. Plus his ass is outstanding."

My father heaved a huge sigh and pilfered some of the pre-lunch cookie dough. I considered stabbing his hand with my fork but that seemed like a little much. I settled for flicking some dough at his forehead.

"Zelda, you sell yourself short," he said as he absently wiped the goop away and licked it from his fingers.

"Oh my Goddess, you just put my spit in your mouth." I shuddered and scrunched my face in disgust.

"Not following you," Dude said in confusion.

"You ate the dough off of your face."

"Yes. And?"

"It came from the fork—which by the way was a weird utensil to hand me to eat dough—that had been in my mouth. Therefore, it stands to reason that some of my saliva was on the fork and most likely the dough that you just ate," I explained.

"So?"

"So you just swallowed my spit. That's gross."

"Zelda, I missed your entire growing up. I never changed your diaper, got spit up on or vomited on by you. I think I'm due a little spit here and there," he said with a wink and a shrug.

I was silent as I shoved more cookie dough in my mouth and wondered why I felt like crying. Naked Dude sat silently and watched. In my weirdly magnanimous mood I offered him some dough off my saliva fork and he gratefully accepted. I watched his Adam's apple bob as he swallowed the raw sugar and spit. Dropping my head into my hands I groaned.

"You're not playing fair. All that stuff about poop and pee and puke is kind of beautifully horrifying," I mumbled through my fingers.

"I'm good that way," Dude said with a gentle smile. "I missed a lot. I can't make up for not being there for you. I also can't say I want to slurp spit on a regular basis, but I would die for you. I fell in love with you the very first day you found me in the dumpster."

"You were kind of hard to avoid," I said as I remembered trying like hell to keep walking past the pitiful mewing on that fated day.

For some unknown reason I stopped and peeked. He was the most mangy and stinky little furball of a cat I'd ever seen. I was repulsed by him, but shockingly it didn't stop me from saving his feline ass. Of course I regretted it daily for the whole two years since. He'd followed me around like a deranged shadow and drove me nuts, but now at least it made more sense why.

I suppose I'd seen something of myself in the odiferous dumpster diver. Both of us were starved for affection and totally alone.

Introspection though was not my forte so I shoved that profound little nugget to the recesses of my brain. This getting to know you crap was becoming messy. I didn't do messy. However, there were some things I wanted to know.

"Did you love my mom?" I asked.

It was a question I'd always pondered. My mom was not very lovable. I loved her—kind of. It was more of a perfunctory thing. All creatures were supposed to love their mothers. However, if the mother didn't love the creature back it became an exercise in futility and a need for therapy as an adult.

Naked Dude put his elbows on the table and put his chin on his palms as he clearly fought for a way to tell me he didn't love her. The thought depressed me, but I had expected no less.

"I thought I did," he said quietly. "I didn't know her very well when we started seeing each other."

"You mean screwing each other," I supplied. No time or need to mince words here.

"Well... um, yes. That would be one way to put it."

"So you did her and left?"

"Not exactly," he hedged. "I honestly didn't know her name the first several times."

I gaped in horror. "You're a total man whore."

"*Was*," he corrected. "I *was* a total man whore. Now I'm simply a warlock who misses licking his balls."

I closed my eyes and pinched the bridge of my nose. The visual he'd just conjured up threatened the contents of my stomach. When he'd been my cat he had an unhealthy obsession with cleaning his nut sack. Clearly it was still an issue.

"All right, let's get back on track here," I muttered. "You nailed her a few times. She got pregnant and you left?"

"Nope."

"Enlighten me," I snapped. As much as I wanted to keep the past in the past, I needed to know.

"Apparently I wasn't the only one *nailing* her. I left when I found out I was one of many," he supplied with a shrug.

"How many?"

"You really want to know?" he asked with a grimace.

"Do I?"

"I'd say no."

"Oh fuck, now I have to know. Let me guess. Tell me if I'm hot or cold," I said. "Four."

"Frigid."

"Eight?"

"Very cold."

"Holy shit... um, twelve?"

"Shivering."

"Motherfucker—pun intended. Twenty five?"

"Cool-ish"

He was correct. I really didn't want to know, but I'd come this far. I wasn't a quitter. And apparently neither was my mother.

"Is it an odd or even number?" I asked needing to narrow the field a little. I was truly on the verge of getting sick.

"It's an odd number ending in five and is ten higher than your last guess," Dude said ending the game before I projectile hurled on him.

"Wait," I said as the circus in my stomach went ballistic. "How do I know you're actually my sperm donor? It could be one of thirty-five," I choked out.

This was not fair. This guy had found me and told me he was my dad. Told me he loved me. And as much as I had no intention of admitting it, he was growing on me. My head spun and my vision narrowed.

"Look at me," Dude demanded as I gulped for air. "Now."

I glanced up from my panic attack and saw a mirror image of myself. It was certainly hard to deny I was his by looks.

My heart slowly stopped hammering in my chest and my breathing returned to normal. I was his. I didn't want to deal with the fact of how happy that made me so I settled for a small smile and a nod.

"You are from a very powerful line of witches. Only our line has red hair and can heal," he said as he took my shaking hand firmly in his. "Our responsibility to our race and others is rather large and somewhat overwhelming. You should have been trained since the time you were a child, but I didn't know. I didn't know you were out there."

"Wait. You're a healer too?" I asked.

"Yes, but the witches in our line are far more powerful than the warlocks."

"So I could kick your ass?" I asked as a smirk pulled at my lips.

"Yes. Yes you could."

Naked Dude chuckled and pulled me close. It felt nice so I let him. Getting used to this sappy shit was dangerous. However, living on the edge was another one of my mottos.

"Are you going to train me?"

"My sister, your Aunt Hildy, would have been so much better, but yes—I will have to suffice."

"I'm not a very good student," I admitted as I disengaged myself and dove back into the cookie dough before I asked him if I could cuddle up on his lap.

"You'll be fine. You've already proven your heart by selflessly healing and defending the Shifters. Controlling the magic is what you need to work on. You have the potential to blow up the continental USA."

My stomach lurched. No one needed that much power and a loose cannon like me had no business possessing that kind of magic. Whatever. It was what it was.

"I should probably change my name to Walking Time Bomb," I mused as I picked the chocolate chips out of the batter. I knew I should stop stuffing my face. I was going to lunch with Mac, but eating kept me from revealing too much of myself to Naked Dude.

"You are no such thing," he chided. "That title belongs to your mother."

"Here's something I don't understand—at your age and with your level of magic, I'm not clear how she was able to put a spell on you. You are one powerful mother humper," I told him.

"Literally or figuratively?" he inquired with a raised eyebrow.

It took me a moment, but when I got it I grinned like an idiot. "Both, I suppose."

Naked Dude considered his answer. His knee bounced and I could literally feel him wracking his brain to come up with an answer that would satisfy me.

"No lies," I insisted.

His head dropped to his chest and he shook it from side to side. He heaved a sigh and then stared at the ceiling. "She said she would harm you unless I dropped my magic and let her do what she wanted."

"She harmed me my whole life," I countered. "Mostly emotionally."

"She never killed you," he replied woodenly.

That certainly shut me the hell up. I mentally calculated how much fucking therapy it was going to take to get rid of the lovely knowledge that my own mother had threatened to kill me.

"Well, that's fanfuckingtastic," I said with a hollow laugh. "Would she have done it?"

"Honestly, I don't know," Dude admitted. "I was not going to take that chance. You're my daughter."

"So you let her turn you into a cat?"

"I wouldn't say *let*... I had no clue what she was going to do," he said as he stood and removed the now empty bowl from in front of me.

"Oh my Goddess. She could have killed you."

The small bit of feeling I had for my mother had now evaporated. She was a monster.

Wrapping my brain around the fact that Fabio would have willingly died for me was more than I could handle. It made me happy, sad and furious all at once. The burning in my gut raced throughout my trembling body. The tablecloth was on fire before I even knew what had happened.

"Shitballs!" I shrieked.

Thankfully Naked Dude was one step ahead and doused the flames with a flick of his hand.

I really *didn't* have control of my magic. Fury was going to either get us all killed or burn my house down.

"Sorry," I mumbled as I quickly sat on my hands. "We should probably start my lessons soon. Like yesterday."

"We will start them tomorrow. I'll tell you all about your Aunt Hildy, and we will figure out how to keep you from being a magical menace," Dude said.

"Do you think the world will be safe from me till then?"

"I certainly hope so. I have a yoga lesson at five."

"Um... that's just weird."

"You think me doing yoga is weird after everything we've just talked about?" he asked as he rinsed the bowl and placed it in the dishwasher.

"Yep, I do."

"My kid says the darndest things," he replied with a delighted smile.

"Oh my Goddess." I groaned and giggled. "You loved saying that, didn't you?"

"Yes. Yes I did."

Chapter 3

Mac looked good enough to eat and smelled like heaven. Dark wavy hair, blue eyes, lashes that belonged on a girl, a body to die for and a face that would make the Goddess weep.

Tall, dark and redonkulously handsome, I was into him like I'd never been into anyone. This of course meant I had to give him a lot of shit. It was unacceptable to let him know how much I liked him—very dangerous for a commitment-phobe loner like me.

"So, pretty girl, you ready for seven today?" Mac asked with a lopsided grin that made me want to jump him and play tonsil hockey.

He leaned on my front door jamb and waited for my answer.

Wait. What the hell was number seven?

I picked imaginary lint off of my dress while I ransacked my brain trying to figure out what he meant. Shit, I knew what sixty-nine was, but seven? Not so much. Should I just pretend I knew what position number seven was or did I come clean? I mean, I wasn't wildly experienced, but I wasn't a virgin either. Was number seven some kind of weird Shifter sex term that I was unaware of?

Son of a bitch. Thirty years on this earth and I had no clue what number seven meant.

"I thought this was number six," Naked Dude remarked sourly as he sat on the couch and pretended to read the paper.

"Holy shit, there's a number six I don't know about too?" I asked bewildered.

Both of the men in my life stared at me as if I was daft.

"You lost me," Mac said.

"Me too," Naked Dude added as he gave Mac the 'evil dad eye'.

"Fairly sure I'm lost too," I mumbled as I tried to push Mac out the front door before we all had to work this one out.

"Oh dear Goddess," Naked Dude choked out, tossing the paper aside and joining us in the foyer. "You thought it was a sexual position?"

"You know what," I groused, as I felt the heat crawl up my neck and land squarely on my cheeks. "Fathers who still wish they could lick their own nads should not talk to their daughters about sex. You are excused from the room. Now."

Fabio slunk away desperately trying not to laugh. I was definitely rethinking my irrational need for a parental unit. I didn't need anyone to embarrass me. I did fine on my own.

"The seventh date," Mac said graciously as put his hand over his mouth to hide his smile. "This is our seventh date of fifteen where no one can die."

"I knew that," I lied without making eye contact.

Mac was sure I was his mate. I considered his claim to be utter bullshit. I was a witch and he was a wolf. Witches mated, but usually with other witches and it wasn't exactly binding. Shifters on the other hand mated for life and we all lived a freakin' long time. I had no plans to blow out puppies. The sexy wolf had repeatedly assured me that this would not be the case. However, I was still investigating.

I was wildly attracted to the bossy, hotter than asphalt in August alpha wolf, but I was also terrified. First of all, the mating ritual involved biting—the kind that broke the skin. While I was down with a little spanky-spanky, biting didn't sound very appealing. Not to mention the fact we didn't really know each other that well.

My solution to the entire matter was that we date each other. He had to take me on fifteen dates where no one died, considering our first date a whole bunch of bad guys died. To be fair, I'd killed most of the bad guys, but it felt like bad karma to start out that way. Fifteen dates also bought me time to run if I couldn't handle it.

"I didn't know that," I admitted sheepishly. "I thought it was some bizarre Shifter sex thing."

"I can certainly make that a reality," Mac said as he ran his thumb along my jaw and raised my chin so our eyes met.

"I'm sure you could," I replied primly and tried not to giggle.

Mac was a freakin' animal in the sack or on the floor or in the shower or on his motorcycle. I hadn't had many lovers, but I was quite sure he'd ruined me for other men.

"So date number seven," I said as I leaned into his warm body.

"Yep, gonna have a good old death-free time."

There wasn't a whole hell of a lot to do in Assjacket, West Virginia and I wondered what he had in mind for our outing.

"Actually, I was thinking we could go to the woods by the river and play Little Red Riding Hood," I suggested. "You know, I say, *'Oh my, what a big tongue you have'*. And then you say, *'The better to lick you with'*."

"Are you sure that's how the story goes?" he inquired with a grin as he copped a feel of my ass and gently pushed me out the front door.

"Yes. Yes, I am positive that's how the story goes."

"That is *NOT* how the story goes," Naked Dude shouted from somewhere upstairs in the house.

"Oh my, what *big* ears you have," I yelled back before I grinned at Mac. "Let's get out of here before he insists on joining us."

Mac shuddered and quickened his pace. "Good thinking, Little Red—very good plan."

***

We did go to the woods, but it wasn't exactly deserted enough for me to start spouting sexed up lines from a fairy tale. Nope. Mac took me to a house in the woods. To be more specific—Mac took me to his house.

It was enormous, a beautiful log cabin with a rustic wraparound porch. It was nestled into the side of a tree-covered hill and looked like it belonged in a magazine. The roof was covered with skylights and I counted at least four chimneys. It was masculine and big—just like its owner. A shiver skittered up my spine. This was getting messy. Messy was bad.

"I'm not sure we know each other well enough for me to see your home," I said as I held my seatbelt shut in the front seat of his monster pick-up truck.

"Zelda, I've been to your place every day for the past few weeks. We've had sex in every room except your father's. It's time to for you to see our house."

He had mumbled the end of the sentence, probably hoping I missed the *our* part... I didn't.

"Can we play Little Red Riding Hood here?" I inquired as I screwed up my courage to get out of the vehicle and see the home of the man I'd been having illicitly spectacular relations with.

"It's not beyond the realm of possibilities," he said with a sexy grin. "But my cook has prepared lunch and I thought I could get you to help me with some ideas for redecorating."

"Very crafty," I congratulated him. "Food and spending money on pretty things. Nice date."

"I thought so," he said as he unsnapped my seat belt and pulled me to him.

His lips grazed my jaw and he buried his face in my neck. Another shiver consumed me, but this one was far more pleasurable.

"Come on," he said as he pulled me out of his truck.

His excitement was cute and somewhat contagious. However, my tummy was flipping like a clogging festival on moonshine. This felt serious. Serious was not part of my repertoire. It reminded me of having to meet the parents of my former boyfriends. Parents never liked me. Of course Mac's parents had died so I couldn't use that excuse for my trepidation.

I had to stall or possibly run. Being that I didn't know the area well, running wasn't my best option. Of course I could always just poof away with a wiggle of my nose or a flick of my hand, but I was trying just to use my magic only for the benefit of others. This was difficult since I was fairly selfish by nature, but I was trying.

"Mac, how long ago did your parents die?" I asked as I bent down to examine a rock, a stick and some colorful fallen leaves.

His smirk revealed he was in on my paranoia. "They died a long time ago. I still miss them."

"How long?" I inquired as I feigned intense interest in a clump of dirt.

"It's been about sixty years," he said.

I froze. Sixty years? How the hell old was the man I'd been playing hide-the-salami with?

"Um, Mac... can I ask you a question?"

"If I say no will that stop you?"

I thought about it for a brief moment. "Probably not."

"Ask away, pretty girl."

Did I want the answer to the question? What if he was as old as my dad? I mean I knew magical races lived for hundreds of years, but this was slightly disconcerting. Shithumpers. To ask or not to ask?

Ask. I always asked. "Exactly how old are you?" I whispered and then held my breath.

"Isn't it rude to ask a person their age?"

"Are you a girl?"

"Not last time I checked," he said as he squatted down next to me.

"Then no, it's not even remotely rude."

"You sure you want the answer, Zelda?"

I thought back to the earlier question I'd asked Naked Dude and the appalling answer I'd received. As I tried to forget the mind-boggling amount of man whores my mother had consorted with, I paused.

Did his age really matter?

No.

Would it change the wildly inappropriate need to slam him to the ground and ride him like a bronco while screaming Yeehaw?

No.

Would it change the alarming fact that I might be falling for the beautiful man next to me?

No.

Would it give me an excuse to get out of something that was way over what I might be able to handle and would surely screw up?

Yes. Yes it would.

"I want to know," I said.

He expelled a slow breath and I tensed.

"I'm seventy-five. I was fifteen when my parents were killed."

Not much rendered me silent, but this did.

Thankfully Mac was not as old as my dad. That would have skeeved me out. Naked Dude was around two hundred years old. However, I was thirty and that made the man I was doing the nasty with forty-five years older than me. The math was heinous. He could be my grandfather if we were human. But we weren't quite human and Mac looked the same age as me. It certainly didn't seem to bother him if the bulge in his jeans was any indication.

"This won't work. We don't have the same pop culture references," I said as I shredded the leaves in my hands.

"I beg to disagree," he shot back. "Favorite bands?"

"Maroon Five, Journey and AC/DC. Yours?"

"Eminem, AC/DC and the Rolling Stones."

"That could possibly work," I muttered. "Favorite TV show?"

"Deadliest Catch," he replied as he settled himself down on the dirt next to me.

I figured he was getting comfortable for what he assumed

would be a long drawn out interrogation.

"I like that one. Would you be willing to watch Project Runway with me?"

"Will it get me laid?"

I looked down so he wouldn't see my grin. He was a total pig and I loved it. "Yes. Yes, it would."

"Then I'm in for a marathon. You hungry?"

"That's an unnecessary question. I'm always hungry," I told him with an eye roll.

Mac stood and extended his hand. I debated taking it. Going inside felt monumental.

"I'm sure lunch is ready. I'd really like you to come inside with me."

I tentatively gave him my hand. "How *much* would you really like it?"

"Sex to Journey's greatest hits and you pick the position *much*."

"Works for me," I said as we slowly walked toward either our future or the end of our relationship.

I was really going to try this commitment thing.

Really really really.

Chapter 4

The interior of the house was gorgeous—all exposed beams, earthy colors and clean lines. However, the *staff* was strange... extremely strange.

"Hello Zelda. My name is Jeeves. I will be at your service today and any other time you require a well-trained valet-cook-butler or even a chaperone to a formal event if Mac is busy off killing things. I studied my craft in England with the Royal Family," said the odd little dude standing in the foyer of Mac's house.

The accent was difficult to pinpoint—kind of British slash Red Neck with a little Australian thrown in for good measure. He was dressed in an ill-fitted tux and tennis shoes and looked to be about twenty years old. Jeeves' long light brown hair was slicked back and braided into at least forty little braids with tiny bows on the end of each. His nails were painted purple and I could swear he was sporting eyeliner. He also had an interesting nervous tic. Jeeves liked to bounce and I found my head bobbing as I watched him.

His smile was gigantic and his welcome was sincere. He was just weird—seriously weird.

This was Mac's cook?

WTF?

"Kyle, what did I tell you about introducing yourself as Jeeves and lying about your credentials?" Mac asked patiently.

"I can't recall," Jeeves mumbled, minus the alarming accent as his bouncing increased in speed and height.

"Kyle... stop," Mac reprimanded as if he were speaking to a

child.

"Well um… I believe you said if I plan on lying I'd better be fucking smart because the truth is a lot easier to remember than the bullshit I usually spout."

"Correct. Would you like to reintroduce yourself to Zelda?" Mac asked.

"Do I have to? The first introduction sounded so much more impressive than the mundane and utterly boring life I lead," Jeeves pouted.

I thought he was going to cry and I almost hugged the little freak. That would simply not do. It was bad enough that the whole town thought I was nice. It would ruin my rep if I became known for compassion too.

"How about this?" I bargained to avoid a blubberfest. "I'll call you Jeeves instead of Kyle if you drop the accent and pony up on some real life facts. Also about the bouncing…"

"He can't help that part. It's in his DNA," Mac cut in quickly. "Kyle is a kangaroo Shifter."

"For real?" I asked, shocked. "I thought they were extinct."

"For the most part we are," Jeeves replied softly. "Mac, the greatest King to grace the round globe of the earth, found me on the side of the road in Australia when I was but a wee, helpless yet adorably precocious joey."

"Really?" I asked as I peeked over at Mac.

I tended to forget my host was the King around here. It was kind of hot to be boffing the King.

"Oh yes," Jeeves went on. "Everyone else thought I was road kill, but not my magnanimous, tremendous, altruistic, benevolent, noble and bighearted savior."

"Clearly Kyle has been reading the thesaurus again," Mac grumbled, uncomfortable with the over the top outpouring of praise. "Let's eat."

He grabbed my hand and tried to pull me to the kitchen, but I wasn't having it.

"So then what happened?" I asked a very talkative Jeeves as I pried my hand from Mac's.

"Why he adopted me of course."

That was certainly something to chew on. If I mated with Mac—not that I had any intention of doing so—I gained a strange little man with an immense vocabulary and a disturbing hair-do?

"So you're his—?" I mumbled not quite sure what term to use.

"I'm his son," Jeeves confirmed. "And I am dearly hoping you will be my mum."

"Um wow," I choked out as I calculated the distance to the front door.

Poofing away would be easier, but it would be a weenie move. I was going to handle this like an adult and run like hell.

"Time to eat," Mac grunted as he yanked my shocked body into the kitchen.

I was lifted into the air and plopped down on a chair. Mac quickly straddled said chair and pinned me so I couldn't head for the hills. Smart man.

"Say something. Now," Mac said as he watched me carefully.

"Ummkay... you're seventy five years old and you have a kangaroo son with an identity crisis who wants me to be his mommy. Is there anything else I should know about you before I kick your ass to the curb?"

His eyes narrowed and my stupid panties dampened with desire. What in the Goddess's name was wrong with me? A deadly werewolf King had me trapped in his kitchen while his bizzarro kangaroo son hopped around the house somewhere. And all I wanted to do was stick my tongue down the wolf's throat and ride him like a cowgirl.

Damn it, I needed to find a new therapist immediately.

"I want you to know this... I have waited seventy-five years for you and I'm not letting you go. Ever. You are mine and I'm yours whether you are ready to accept it or not. As for Kyle, he was dying on the side of a road and no one wanted him. I took him and had to adopt him so he would legally be under my protection."

"It's Jeeves, not Kyle," the bouncing weirdo shouted from the foyer.

"Go outside and play," Mac yelled back.

"I never get to stay for the good stuff," Jeeves whined.

"Now," Mac demanded.

"Going," Jeeves answered dejectedly.

Jeeves slammed the front door behind him bitching like a pre-pubescent girl. I closed my eyes and pinched the bridge of my nose.

Did I want to leave? Nope. I was clearly insane.

Should I leave? Yes. I was very ill equipped for this adventure that was playing out. I was barely capable of taking care of myself.

However, the sex was so damn good, I decided to hear him out.

Shallow? Yes.

Did I care? Not so much.

"Keep talking, little mister," I said as I narrowed my own eyes right back at him.

"I have no more secrets like Kyle. I was worried about your reaction. He's harmless and can cook like a pro chef—plus he's grown on me over time."

"He lives here?" I asked as I noticed the mouthwatering aroma coming from the stove.

"Yes, he does."

"That kind of fucks up playing Little Red Riding Hood... vague pun intended," I informed him as I covertly glanced over at the stove.

"Hungry?" he asked with a smirk.

Maybe I wasn't so covert. "Possibly," I replied as his scent mixed with the food hit my nose. I was in Nirvana times ten.

"How about this. I will remove myself from your hot bod and feed you if you promise not to run," Mac suggested warily as he ran his hand through his dark hair.

"What about poofing away?"

"No poofing either. Deal?" he asked.

"What's for lunch?" I inquired and wanted to punch my own head for being so easily bought.

"Coq au vin, steamed potatoes, homemade crusty French bread and molten chocolate lava cake with vanilla ice cream for dessert. Also homemade," Jeeves announced with his face plastered to the screen of the open kitchen window.

"I told you to go outside and play," Mac snapped.

"I am outside," Jeeves reasoned.

"He is outside," I admitted with a grin.

Mac's frustration with his son was getting amusing. But to be fair, Jeeves was a pain in the ass.

"Go play then," Mac ground out.

"Fine. I'll play, but I'd like to go on record that this is incredibly unfair treatment. I'm an outstanding conversationalist and a sought after dinner partner."

"So noted," Mac said. "Play. Now. Far away from the house."

We sat in silence and stared at each other. It was all I could do not to laugh. Squirming beneath him, I felt evidence of his desire for me and it made my head spin. It would just figure that I was nuts for a werewolf with baggage.

"I'll stay for lunch," I said as I pressed up against his erection.

His quick intake of breath was hot—very hot—almost hot enough to make me forgo lunch, but food was food and I was always hungry. Plus the thought of Jeeves popping up at an inappropriate moment dampened my immediate need for sex just a bit.

"After lunch we'll play," Mac promised as he began heaping food onto plates.

"What about Jeeves?"

Mac paused, sighed and then grinned. "I'll send him to the grocery. He loves the grocery. He'll be gone for hours."

"I heard all of that," Jeeves yelled from the yard.

"Of course you did," Mac muttered as he shook his head.

"Maybe it's time Jeeves got his own apartment," I whispered since the kangaroo had super sonic hearing.

"You might have a point there," Mac replied. "A very fine point."

Chapter 5

"Oh my Goddess," I moaned as I patted my full tummy. "Jeeves can definitely cook."

"Told ya," Mac replied as he polished off the rest of the lava cake.

Thankfully Jeeves had gone to the grocery. He was so excited to shop for food his hopping reached levels that almost made my neck cramp from trying to maintain eye contact with him.

"So what do you want to do now?" I asked as I leaned forward in my chair to give Mac a nice view of my cleavage.

His stare was downright lascivious and I giggled.

"I'm thinking it's story time."

"Which story would you like to hear?" I asked as I leaned a little further.

"The one where we end up naked and rolling around in the sheets," he replied in a low sexy rumble that made me shiver.

"Not sure I know that one," I teased.

"Oh, I think you'll enjoy it. A lot."

"Possibly. I suppose there's only one way to find out. Oh, and I brought props," I said as I reached down and ransacked my purse.

"Lay them on me," Mac said pulling his shirt over his head and tossing it on the floor.

Sweet Goddess Almighty, I paused and took in the scenery with a huge grin. No one had the right to look like he did. His six-pack was actually an eight-pack and the light sprinkling of hair on his chest that veed down to my favorite part of his body made my fingers itch to touch him.

"It has to be in the bedroom to do it right," I explained as I got back to business and found what I was searching for.

I tossed him a granny cap and then dug around my bag for elastic hair ties. My locks were fire red, not golden, but I figured I could whip my mass of curls into pigtails for a more realistic approach.

"Bedrooms are up... Wait. What the hell is this?" Mac asked as he gingerly held up the white granny cap as if it were a dead mouse. "You cannot expect me to put this on my head. My Johnson will not be okay with this. At all."

"Trust me. I'll make sure your Johnson is just fine and you have to wear it. It's the rules. However, we need to discuss the name of your thingie. I was thinking we should call him Bon Jovi or Adam Levine."

"Absolutely not," Mac snapped, instinctually protecting his dangly parts with his hands. "He's been Johnson for as long as I can remember."

"Well that's certainly a long time, considering you're older than dirt," I shot back.

I thought I'd come up with creative names. His shooting down my suggestions for renaming his penis didn't bode well for a healthy relationship.

Mac's bark of laughter made me roll my eyes.

"Fine. You can call him Johnson and I'll call him Petey," I said with a shrug.

"Whoa, whoa, whoa. What happened to Bon Jovi?" he demanded realizing he might be losing quickly.

"I thought you didn't like Bon Jovi."

"Well it's certainly better than Petey," he huffed.

"Fine Bon Jovi it is," I said as I stood up, finished my girly hair do and yanked my dress over my head. "Put on your cap. You have to get under the covers and pull them up to your nose. I will then enter the room and we can just improvise."

My barely there panties and sheer bra clearly made the new moniker for his wank forgotten news. Men were so easy.

"I will be naked under the covers," he announced, daring me to disagree as he eyed me like prey.

"Well, duh. Of course you will," I told him as I sprinted from the room looking for the stairs. "Put on the cap or Bon Jovi will be singing the blues," I yelled over my shoulder.

The house was huge and I got lost as I searched for the stairs. Where in the hell were they? Of course I could stop running in circles and simply ask Roger the rabbit.

WTF?

What was Roger rabbit doing here? Had Mac lied? Was the bizarre and somewhat rude rabbit Shifter his freakin' son too?

"Good afternoon, Zelda," Roger choked out with large eyes as he took in my attire or rather lack there of.

"I'd hesitate to use the word good, Roger. Close your eyes," I demanded.

He did. Reluctantly—but he did.

"Now where in the hell are the stairs in this house?" I snapped.

"Down the hallway and on the left," he informed me. "Can I open my eyes now?"

"Nope. Next question. What are you doing here?"

"Who are you talking to?" Mac asked as he rounded the corner and stopped short when he spied a closed eyed Roger.

"I'm speaking to Roger rabbit and if he's another one of your sons, I'm out of here. I don't care how big your Bon Jovi is. This is not worth it."

"He's *not* my son," Mac said. "I only have one."

The silence was slightly awkward. Unfortunately, Roger decided to fill it.

"So you call your man rod Bon Jovi?" Roger asked with a shit-eating grin.

If looks could kill, I'd be dead from the one Mac was giving me.

"That's really none of your business," I quickly informed the nosy little assmunch. I actually felt guilty that I'd outed Mac's penis' new name to the town gossip. Everyone would know five minutes after Roger left.

Time to fix my blunder. "Please tell me you did not use the term *man rod* for a weenie."

"Um… maybe," Roger mumbled as his cheeks flamed red.

"Interesting. So, ahhh… clearly you watch a lot of porn. I wonder if everyone in town is aware of your hobby?" I said hoping I was onto something.

"Well, I… you see, I…" Roger stuttered.

Bullseye. I was definitely onto something.

"Wow, it would be really difficult to show your face at picnics if all the ladies in town knew you watched other people hump and moan twelve hours a day—fourteen on the weekends. But maybe everyone already knows," I said as I watched him quake in his little rabbit boots.

Roger's face had gone ashen and I felt kind of bad, but a girl had to protect her man's wanker's reputation. However, the rabbit looked like he might puke. If he puked, I would puke and I wanted to be Little Red Fucking Riding Hood. Time to end my game and win.

"How about this, Roger?" I offered as Mac watched me with raised brows and arms crossed over his ridiculously muscled chest. "You forget you ever heard the term Bon Jovi in association with Mac's *man rod* and I forget that you watch porn twenty-four seven. Deal?"

"You really wouldn't say anything?" he asked in a small voice.

"Witch's Honor," I assured him.

I was still kind of shocked and completely grossed out that he watched so much porn. I'd pulled that one right out of my butt. Thank the Goddess I'd been correct.

"I never heard a word," Roger swore fervently. "In fact, I'm pretty sure I was never even here today at all."

"Which brings me back to my last question. What in the hell *are* you doing here?" I asked.

"Can I open my eyes?" he inquired casually.

Way too casually.

"No," Mac hissed as he revealed his possessive alpha self. "If you open your eyes I will gouge them out."

"That's not very hospitable, sweetie," I said as I pulled down my panties and showed him my left butt cheek.

"Roger, get to your point *now*," Mac shouted, obviously in sexually frustrated hell.

"Um… of course," Roger choked out as he trembled like a leaf. "I was here to inquire about Zelda's progress with the evil that lurks in our area."

"Right now Roger, you are the only evil that lurks," I informed him as Mac mooned me.

I bit back my giggle and realized Roger was still here and waiting for an answer. That sobered me.

Roger had a legit question. Not only was I the new Shifter Wanker, the go-to gal for fixing Shifter booboos, I was bound by honor to keep the magical balance and eliminate any danger in my area. Unfortunately there was danger in my area.

My Aunt Hildy, the former Shifter Whisperer, had been murdered in the most horrific way by honey badger Shifters. They'd used a blue liquiform solution to render her magic-less then had extracted her power with a huge, glowing syringe. Then they injected my aunt's magic into the head honey badger. Sadly, the way I knew this was their rubbery bastard leader had projected the horrid images into my mind right before I blew up his entire colony.

They were vying for power and by killing my aunt, they'd created chaos amongst the Shifters. The ugly bastard was smart, but not quick enough to outsmart me.

I left only him alive. After punching my fist into his chest—which was *beyond* fucking gross—I took back my aunt's magic and turned him over to the Witch Council. Baba Yaga, our slightly insane yet mostly fair leader, and her crew of icky older-than-the-beginning-of-time warlocks had taken him away. They had not been able to get any information out of the ugly bastard. That surprised me greatly. The Council was feared and revered for their rather unconventional methods of torture.

I'd been waiting for guidance from Baba Yodorkmamma and the Council, but since none was forthcoming it was time to get to work without them. Roger the cock-blocker had an excellent point along with having tremendously bad timing. I had a job to do and I wasn't doing it.

"It's stalled at the moment," I admitted to Roger.

His eyes flew open in shock and Mac tackled him ready to remove his peepers.

"No! Down boy," I shouted. "Roger was not ogling my boobs. Were you Roger?"

"Um..." he mumbled.

"You were *not* ogling my boobs," I told him hoping he would play along. Clearly the little pervert was ogling my boobs, but I would hate to try to heal eyes that had been separated from his body. The migraine I would get would preclude me from sexual activity for weeks.

"Mac, if you plan on getting laid this month, you will stop manhandling Roger."

"Close your eyes," Mac ground out to a whimpering Roger. "I am the only one who is allowed to see her naked."

"I'm not exactly naked," I told him.

"Well, pretty much," Roger chimed in and received a swift punch to the head.

"Roger, I'd suggest you zip it. Mac is a teeny weensy bit possessive and I think you'd like to keep your eye balls in their sockets," I said as I pulled Mac off of him.

"Yes, yes of course," Roger stammered as he got up and ran. However, since his eyes were shut he hit the wall three times. He then knocked over two end tables and more than likely gave himself a slight concussion when he nailed the wrought iron coat stand before he made it out the front door.

His timing was not good, but his point was well made. I'd been avoiding finding the syringe and solution because I was happy for the first time in my life. Going after *the evil that lurked* was likely to end my new and cozy little life.

Wouldn't it just figure that I'd finally found my father and a guy who actually liked my crazy and I had to probably die by finding the lurking fucking evil? So. Not. Fair.

"You are not going after the evil alone," Mac said as he came up behind me and put his strong arms around me.

"Oh my Goddess, can you read my mind?" I demanded, alarmed that maybe he had more secret powers than I could deal with.

"Nope, your face. You're very expressive."

"You don't think I can do it alone?" I huffed indignantly as I extricated myself from his embrace.

He paused and stared. "I think you are capable of anything you put your mind to," he said slowly. "But, you don't have to go it alone anymore—or ever again."

Son of a bitch, first Naked Dude made me want to cry because he swallowed my spit and now Mac wasn't playing fair. No one had ever had my back. I'd always been on my own. I was swimming in the deep end without my ducky life-preservers. This was getting more dangerous than the evil that lurked. Shitballs on fire.

"Okay, here's the deal," I said, swallowing back my tears as I made a plan that would temporarily postpone the inevitable. "Since there's a fine chance that you or I or the entire town may die tomorrow when we go after the asscranking evil, I say we have sex five times today. Twice with the granny cap and three without. We forget about anything except massive orgasms and then eat some of Jeeves' leftovers. Deal?"

"No deal," Mac said as he put the granny cap on his head. "We have sex eight times—four with the granny cap and four without."

"Do we get to eat afterward?" I inquired liking the revision.

"I'll be eating the entire time, but I can always make room for some food."

"You are a total pig," I squealed with delight.

"Nope, I'm a wolf and I have a big tongue, Little Red Riding Hood."

My knees practically buckled, my nipples hardened to the point of pain and I made a sound that belonged in one of Roger's beloved porno flicks. If I didn't decide to be a wussy and leave town because everything was too good to be true, or if I didn't die in the next few days, I was so keeping Mac. Any man who would wear a granny cap, let me call his wanker Bon Jovi, made me lose my balance, and had a certifiably insane son who could win Iron Chef was a keeper.

"I like your terms. However, we are going to my place. I will not run the risk of letting Jeeves see you defile me dressed like an old woman. Plus my place is empty. Naked Dude is going to yoga at five."

"Put your clothes back on. Now," Mac insisted as he dragged me back to the kitchen. "If anyone sees you dressed like this, I'll have to rearrange their face and I don't have time for that today."

"For once I've got no problem with your bossy request," I said as I quickly dressed. His Neanderthal ways were actually growing on me—not that I would ever let him know. "No problem at all."

Chapter 6

"What the hell?" Mac shouted as he slammed the truck into park.

Mac's pick-up bucked and jerked as we ran over something large.

"Oh shit," I screeched. "What in the Goddess' name did we just back over?"

I blanched and had a sickening deja vu of backing over and killing Naked Dude when he had been my cat. Shitshitdamnshit. Had Roger passed out from a concussion and we'd just flattened him? If we had, I was going to have a bitch of a time healing that level of damage.

I white knuckled the dash and said a quick Hail Mary even though I wasn't even remotely Catholic.

Mac was out of the truck before I even had my seatbelt off. Damn, wolves were fast. In my panic to free myself I got completely tangled in the strap. I couldn't move. Wait. What the hell was I thinking? I'm a witch, damn it. With a quick flick of my fingers, the seatbelt disintegrated to dust and I was out of the passenger seat.

I was terrified until I took in the scene and then I was just pissed. How many more hairy buttball Shifters were going to mess with my sex life?

"Get out from under the truck, Chuck," I ground out through clenched teeth. "I only have an hour to get through the entire story of Little Red Riding Hood eight times and you are fucking that up. Pun intended."

"Not following you," Chuck grunted as he eased his

enormous frame out from under the back wheels and knocked Mac's monster truck over in the process. This was unbelievable. I refused to kill Chuck, but I was going to make it difficult for him to sit for a few days. A nice electrical zap to his backside should do the trick.

"My god, man," Mac said as he helped Chuck to his feet. "I'm so sorry. I didn't see you behind me."

"Of course you didn't," I snapped. "Because Chuck was hiding under the wheel wanting you to mow his idiot ass down. Isn't that correct, Chuck?"

Chuck grinned and shrugged. "You got me pegged, Zelda."

"Okay," Mac said as he pressed his temples. "Now, I'm not following."

I glared at Chuck who didn't appear to be forthcoming with an explanation. Shaking my head and yanking on my pigtails, I slowly blew out a long breath. I was this close to making Chuck's death wish come true. That would be terribly wrong. I could end up back in the magic pokey, which would suck, and I liked Chuck. Not so much at the moment... but generally speaking.

"Chuck here is trying to off himself. I don't know why and he won't tell me because he could end up naked in a black hole somewhere," I explained to a now very befuddled Mac.

"It's actually a time warp with elevator music," Chuck corrected me.

"Whatever," I yelled as a colorful burst of flame flew from my fingertips narrowly missing Chuck's smiling and very handsome face. "I do not have time for this. I am supposed to have the big O eight times before I bite the big one tomorrow."

"How are you going to do that?" Chuck inquired with interest.

"Seriously?" I asked.

"Yes."

"Well, um... okay. I'm going to put on a red cape over only my bra and panties and Mac is going to wear a granny cap. He's going to be naked under the covers and pretend to be the Big Bad Wolf. And then I'm going to..."

"No, no, no, no, no," Chuck gasped out trying unsuccessfully not to laugh.

Mac began to walk in tight circles shaking his head.

"Not that part," Chuck said with a chuckle and a wink to a mortified Mac. "I get that part. Well, kind of... the granny cap is a little unsettling. I was talking about the 'bite it' part. How are you going to do that?"

"I'm done," I snapped. "You will tell me right now why

35

you're trying to kill yourself."

"Can't," Chuck replied.

"Won't," I shot back.

"That too," he agreed with a smile.

This was bullshit. I marched right over to the cryptic bear and smacked his arm. Chuck and I stood nose to nose. Well actually we stood with my nose to his belly button because he was at least seven feet tall. However, I was not backing down. It was time for the big oaf to come clean.

"Color me clueless," Mac cut in.

"With a sexually frustrated Bon Jovi," I added.

"Not helping, Little Red," Mac said.

"Sorry," I muttered and made a silent zip the lip motion.

"What does Bon Jovi have to do with anything?" Chuck asked.

Now we were all confused.

"Nothing," I said quickly. "Bon Jovi has nothing to do with anything at all. Ever. Nothing. Not a thing."

"Your lips are zipped," Mac reminded me with a huge sigh. "Do not say anything else. Please."

I gave him a weak thumbs up and backed away from Chuck a bit so I wouldn't feel so inclined to put my two cents in every other word. Hard, but doable. Maybe.

"Chuck," Mac said. "You have some explaining to do. Has something happened? It's against the laws of nature and our people to kill yourself. As your King, I forbid it."

Chuck went to his knees before Mac and stared straight up at him. An intensity that I could feel passed between the two men and I watched in fascination. It was starkly beautiful and I felt completely left out. We're they talking? I strained to hear, but leaves rustling in the wind were the only sound in the air.

Dang it, was this another Shifter thingie?

"I understand," Mac said quietly to Chuck as he placed his hand on the bear's head. "But you have to understand that our community is in danger right now and I need you. You are one of my strongest fighters. Until the threat is contained or gone, I will not give you my blessing to leave us. Are we clear?"

Chuck looked pained, but nodded respectfully. "Yes, Sire. You have my word."

I was dying here. I hated not being in on the secret, but I'd bet every bit of uncontrolled magic I had that no one was going to make me any wiser. Crap.

However, there was one thing I wanted clarified.

"Can I speak?" I burst out, louder than I intended as both men jumped.

"Apparently you can," Mac said with a grin. "And no, I can't tell you anything."

"I know," I griped. "That's not what I want to ask. Well, it is, but I won't."

"Uh huh," Mac said with raised brows and a skeptical look on his face.

"Seriously," I promised. "I can respect private stuff—kind of. But I don't get something," I said to Chuck.

"What's that?" Chuck inquired as he carefully righted Mac's truck.

"I thought you had to bite the bullet at my house. Was that a lie?"

"No," Chuck explained. "It would be better is I did it there, but now I figure as long as I do it near you everything would work out just fine."

"Let me get this straight," I said not liking where this was going. "You're telling me that if I live through taking care of the lurking fucking evil, I have watching you off yourself as something to look forward to?"

"It sounds kind of depressing when you put it that way," Chuck said, scratching his head.

"Is there another way to put it?" I demanded.

"Um… none I can think of," he replied and gave me a quick hug. "And just so you know, I call mine Superman."

"You call your what Superman?" I asked.

Chuck was weird and clearly unbalanced.

"My Bon Jovi," he informed Mac and me with a loud guffaw as he loped off into the woods. "Oh, and I stopped by your house and fixed the fridge. Made a little mess, but I cleaned it up."

At least he hadn't offed himself. It would suck massive donkey balls to go home to that.

"Thanks." I yelled after him.

"No, problem," he said still laughing as he disappeared into the tree line.

"Shit," I mumbled as I stared up at the sky. "I should have left well enough alone. Johnson wasn't that bad."

"You figure?" Mac asked with a smirk.

"Yessssssssss," I said. "However, since the word is out, I'm sticking with Bon Jovi."

"Fine," he said way too agreeably. "What do you call yours?"

I gaped at him and tried to think fast on my feet. My woowoo didn't actually have a name. I'd never been vain or stupid enough to name her.

"Um…"

"I was thinking either Katie Couric or Miley Cyrus," he suggested while he casually dusted off his truck.

Sweet Mother of the Goddess. I had no come back. I was so confused about the connection between Katie Couric and Miley Cyrus that I was totally mute. Plus, I was not naming my vajayjay after a morning news anchor or a twerker with a two-foot tongue.

What to do... what to do... what to do...

"Ummmm..."

"Or how about Queen Elizabeth?" he suggested mildly as he continued to check his fucking truck for damage.

"Do you hate me?" I shouted as I plopped down on the ground and sat on my hands. I was so wound up, I was worried I would zap him or blow his pick up to smithereens.

I was not naming my girlie parts any of those names. Ever. If I had to pick one I'd pick Little Red Riding Hood, but that was entirely too long to yell in the throws of passion. Plus I would laugh.

"Not even a little bit," Mac said grinning from ear to ear.

If he wasn't so stupidly handsome, I'd smite the smile right off his face.

"Okay, fine," I said in defeat. "You can call your *man rod* Johnson."

"Nope, I'll stick with Bon Jovi."

"What exactly does that mean for my vahooha?" I asked, terrified of the potential answer.

"I suppose we could go with Little Red Riding Hood," he replied with a smirk.

"Oh my hell," I cried out. "You *can* read minds."

"Only a mind that talks as loud as yours does."

"What have I gotten myself into?" I muttered as I stood up and let him take his chances with my erratic magic.

"A whole lot of trouble and a whole lot of fun."

I stared at the beautiful man in front of me for a long moment. What really sucked and scared me the most was that he was as gorgeous on the inside as he was on the outside. His people respected him. He'd adopted a freak because no one else would take him. He was kind and fair and hotter than Satan's boxer briefs. And the simple fact that he could put up with me was making me let my guard down. Not smart—not smart at all.

Of course, I didn't buy the whole 'I'm your mate' thing, but mate or not I was falling fast and hard. I never fell fast and hard... I never fell at all.

Too much introspective thought was giving me a headache. Luckily I knew a sure cure for a headache. Eight big O's.

"Alrighty then," I said reasonably. If I couldn't beat him, I should probably get laid. "Let's go to my house and introduce Little Red Riding Hood to Bon Jovi."

"Sounds like a plan, sexy girl."

"If we hurry we can get to the part of the story where I say, 'Oh my! What a big Bon Jovi you have' and then you can say… "

"Um, Zelda?"

"Yes?"

"I definitely know what to say then."

"Oh, okay. Then let's go. And make sure Chuck didn't sneak back here and wedge his big fat bear ass under the hood. That would activate my gag reflex."

"Roger that, sexy. Get in the car. Now."

"You're awfully bossy," I said with a grin.

"Yep, Big Bad Wolves are very bossy," he answered as he slapped my butt and put me in the truck. "You got a problem with that?"

"Not today, Hot Stuff. Definitely not today."

Chapter 7

"Let's go to my room and get ready," I said as I slammed the front door behind us and took the stairs two at a time. "Strip and put on the cap. We clear?"

"Yep," Mac said from behind me as he scooped me up and took the stairs three at a time. "You actually have a red cape?"

"I do," I squealed gleefully as he tossed me onto the bed and began to quickly remove his clothes. "It's Chanel. Fabio procured it for me. Wouldn't he just have a fit if he knew what I was wearing it for?"

"I'd have to say yes to that." Mac chuckled and continued to strip. "Should I shift?"

"Um, no. That would be kind of weird," I said as I fastened the cape and adjusted my pigtails.

"I thought we were playing Little Red Riding Hood."

He stopped undressing and stood half naked and perplexed in the middle of my bedroom.

"Operative word being *play*," I explained as I considered jumping his partially clad body and having my way with him. No. That would ruin the game and I already had on my costume.

"But wouldn't it be more realistic if I shifted into my wolf?" he asked.

"Do you want to get laid?" I inquired as I popped on some fabu red stilettos that Naked Dude had probably shop lifted for me.

"What kind of question is that?" Mac demanded as he gestured to his painfully erect Bon Jovi.

"A legit one. Big hairy things on four legs do not get laid by witches in red capes. Hot studs with nice Bon Jovis do. Period."

"*Nice?*" he yelled. "You think my Bon Jovi is *nice?*"

"Oh my hell," I muttered under my breath. "I meant ginormous, magical and the best I've ever had in my life."

"Thank you."

"You're welcome. Now get in the bed," I instructed, trying not to giggle. Mac was putty in my hands. Well actually steel, but...

"You do realize that my Bon Jovi is the only one you will be allowed to look at, touch or play with ever again," he informed me in a brook-no-bullshit alpha tone.

"You do realize you just referred to your *man rod* as Bon Jovi," I shot back wanting to avoid the whole mating issue. I wanted to have sex, not an argument about his archaic beliefs.

"I'm getting used to it," he said. "And you are avoiding it."

"I would never avoid your Bon Jovi," I said quickly as I opened my cape hoping to distract him with my boobs.

He was moving too fast. I wasn't a Shifter. I was a witch and a commitment-phobe to boot. The whole mating thing was alarming. I'd never kept a boyfriend for longer than a month. He was smoking crack to think I could give him a lifetime no matter how spectacular his Bon Jovi was.

"You're avoiding your fate," he said.

"I thought fate was unavoidable," I said with an eye roll.

"It is," he said smugly. "Which is why I haven't chained you up in my house."

Speechless. The gorgeous idiot kept rendering me speechless. I decided to ignore the dumbass part of my brain that was turned on by being chained up by a Neanderthal werewolf. Better to deal with it in therapy. I desperately needed to find a damn therapist.

"I shall make a conscious effort to ignore your he-man tendencies and proceed with my x-rated fairy tale. However, you and your Bon Jovi are skating on some thin ice at the moment and my fingers are itching to zap your butt."

"Goddess, you're hot," he growled as he hopped naked into the bed, granny cap and all.

It was wildly difficult to argue when all I wanted to do was laugh. He was going to increase my already abundant insanity and I really didn't care. The beautiful, sexy asshead made me happy. Happy was a new place for me—frightening and overwhelming—but all kinds of wonderful.

"Here's the deal," I said laying out the groundwork. "Since we're doing improv with this puppy, I'm going to scream in terror, stumble very sexily over to the bed and fall on top of you.

I'll pretend like it was an accident and maybe my cape will fall off or possibly my panties. You can start saying some of the lines I suggested earlier and then we do it. Cool?"

"Are you supposed to plan an improv?" he asked as he pressed his lips together to keep from grinning.

"Technically, no," I admitted sheepishly. "But... I've kind of planned this one out a little."

"Works for me," he said in a voice that made my panties dampen.

He crooked his finger and beckoned me over. "Come a little closer, my dear."

"Oh my, what big eyes you have," I said as I unhooked my cape for easier access.

"The better to see you with," he growled seductively. "I have a few other big things that might interest you too."

"Really?" I asked as I bit down on my tongue to stifle my laugh. "What ever do you mean?"

"It's better if you come see," he purred. "Much better."

"Well, since I forgot my glasses, I should probably get really close," I told him as seriously as I could.

I thought that was a fantastic line. I impressed myself with my improv abilities. I briefly wondered if Assjacket had a community theatre.

I stumbled for real as he pulled down the covers and revealed a body that should belong to a Greek god. Cape, shoes, bra, panties and Mac's granny cap disappeared and flew across the room with a magical flick of my fingers. His hiss sent my newly named Little Red Riding Hood into overdrive and I dove on him like I was competing on the Olympic swim team. I expected our romp to be wild and out of control.

I couldn't have been more wrong or in deeper water. Mac flipped me, pinned my naked body beneath his and then he stilled. His lids were heavy and his breathing was labored. My tummy tingled and my brain sent off warning signals to my entire body. The intensity of the moment was too much—way too much.

"What are you doing?" I demanded, staring at his collarbone. His eyes were telling me a story I wasn't ready to hear. "This was *not* in the script."

"I was under the impression this was an improv," Mac replied as his large hands began to gently caress my face, my shoulders, my hips and my stomach. "Your skin is so soft," he murmured as his lips followed the trail his hands had taken.

"We're supposed to do the nasty," I insisted as a lump formed in my throat.

"We will," he promised. "I just want to worship you a little bit."

"I'm really not worthy," I tried to tell him, but he was having none of it.

It was as sexy as sex itself. No one had ever simply touched me. Men had always gone straight for the boobs or the Little Red Riding Hood. This felt so good and so right I was tempted to smite his ass. Damndamndamn. This alpha assmonkey was going to break me. And I was probably going to let him.

But not quite yet.

With a little burst of sparkling golden magic I levitated us into the air and rolled on top of him. His delighted chuckle was music in to my ears. He wasn't afraid of me even though I could blow up Assjacket along with the rest of the USA. He liked my crazy, my shoulders, my magic *and* my boobs.

"Is this in the script?" he asked as his full lips brushed mine and he pulled my hips to meet his.

"Kind of," I said as a slow sensual burn began to coil in my stomach. "This is kind of a mixture of Little Red Riding Hood and Peter Pan… with the flying and all."

"I like it," he said as his teeth scraped my neck.

I shuddered and lost a bit of control, which resulted in us plopping back down on the bed with a thud.

"Oh sweet Goddess on High, this is like a movie. You know, one with Kate Winslet or Reese Witherspoon, but with some raunchy voodoo woowoo thrown in. I need some caramel popcorn and a vodka," Mac said in a high feminine voice.

Wait. WTF? Had I kneed him in the nuts and made him a soprano?

Had I accidentally shoved his balls up into his body and turned him into a girly man who liked Kate Winslet and caramel popcorn?

Holy Hell, I was a fucking magical menace.

"Um, that's really weird. Did I squash your nads?" I asked.

"No, why do you ask?" Mac, back in normal voice, replied.

"Well, when you mentioned Kate Winslet, Reese Witherspoon and popcorn in a girly voice."

"What are you talking about?" he asked completely confused.

"You just said this was like a movie and then you said raunchy voodoo woowoo," I accused.

What kind of weird game was he playing? Maybe this was good. Maybe he was crazier than me and I could legally kick him to the curb and blow this town. Well, not blow as in blow up—just get the hell out.

Except I didn't want to kick him to the curb. And I didn't want to leave.

So the fuck what if he liked to pretend he was a girl every so often? As long as his Bon Jovi could still make me lose brain cells, who was I to judge?

And as long as he didn't want to wear my panties and insist I pretend I'm a dude this could still possibly work.

"Zelda, I have never uttered the words raunchy voodoo woowoo in my life," Mac said as he sat up and gave me an odd look.

"You didn't say that?" I asked as I sat up too.

"Nope and I didn't hear a thing," he added watching me carefully.

Shit. Was I losing it?

"Well I heard it," I told him as I pulled the covers around me. This was not going as planned. My having a psychotic break was fucking up my fairy tale.

"*Of course you heard it,*" a musical feminine voice trilled. "*Because I said it.*"

"What the..." I muttered as I glanced wildly around the room searching for the body that belonged to the voice.

"What's going on?" Mac asked as he pulled me against him and prepared to shift.

"Cover your Bon Jovi. We have company and it's a female. I will not have any woman looking at your thingie except me," I snapped.

His wide grin made me want to smack my own head off. I sounded as possessive as him. Not good.

"I don't see anyone," he said as he scanned the room.

"Me neither, but we definitely have a guest. Show yourself," I shouted as I waved my hand and promptly re-dressed Mac and myself in the clothing that littered the floor of my bedroom.

"*You have to guess my name,*" she said accompanied by a somewhat deranged laugh.

I rolled my eyes and sighed. Apparently orgasms were not in the cards for me today. I was not even remotely afraid of the body-less spirit in my room. The nutty woman's presence wasn't threating.

Annoying? Yes.

Deadly? Absolutely not.

"Oh my hell," I said wearily. "If I guess your name, will you leave?"

"*Maybe,*" she said.

I bet she was lying through her teeth... if she had teeth. Who knew what she even was? Was she a person? An animal? A ghost? A demon?

Mac stayed at attention, ready to shift and kill at a moment's notice. Goddess, he was hot.

"Oookay, fine. Is your name Rumplefuckinstiltskin?" I inquired in rather impolite tone.

"*Nope!*"

"Coitus Interruptus?"

"*Nope!*" she shot back gleefully.

"Pain in my ass?" I snapped. This could go on for days.

"*Now that's just rude,*" she pouted.

"But you barging in on my somewhat immoral out of wedlock escapades in a red cape and pigtails isn't?" I shot back.

"*Oooooooo.*" She gasped in excitement and joy as her invisible hands clapped loudly. "*Are you going to marry him?*"

WTF? She was grinding my very last nerve. If I could just find her, I could zap her mouth shut followed by a nice stinging ass zinger.

"First of all, that is none of your business. Secondly, Shifters don't get married. They bite each other with long, sharp, pointy teeth—which by the way is barbaric. No marriage. They mate and probably bleed profusely in the fucking process," I informed her with a shudder. "They mate. For life. No outs. No sex with anyone other than the hairball who scarred you permanently with his canines. Add to the list the possibility of blowing puppies out of my woohooha and being stuck in Assjacket, West Virginia for the rest of my years. Not to mention all the shedding and clogged vacuum cleaners—not that I vacuum."

I realized I was hyperventilating, but that didn't seem to stop my mouth from working. Mac watched me warily like I was a time bomb waiting to go off. Smart man. He'd be smarter to run.

"Oh my Goddess," I shouted as I gasped for air. "Mac, you have to leave or move or find another mate. Now!"

"Zelda, it's all good," Mac replied calmly as he smoothed the wild curls that had escaped my pigtails behind my ears. "Shifters can get married if that's what you want."

"That's not what I want," I screeched. "All I want is eight orgasms and a brief cuddle. All of you freaks in Assjacket are trying to change me into a responsible person who cares. This is *not* what I signed up for."

"*She really did a number on you,*" the voice whispered sadly.

"Who did a number on me?" I demanded.

"*Why your mother, of course. She's a horrible woman.*"

"Leave my mother out of this," I huffed.

"I didn't mention your mother," Mac said.

"Not you. Her."

"Your mother's here?" he asked totally confused.

"Shit, I certainly hope not."

"You still haven't guessed my name," the disembodied voice chimed in completely ignoring my mental collapse.

"I heard that," Mac whispered as he got to his knees and sniffed the air.

"See, I'm not crazy," I said.

"Never thought you were," he said.

"Don't try to butter me up by saying nice things," I informed him. "You still have to find a new mate."

"Whatever you say, baby," he replied.

Hmmmm… that was not an answer. However, there was an irritating presence still wafting around my room somewhere that needed to be dealt with before I argued about it.

"Well, shit on a stick. I'm losing my touch. Only Zelda was supposed to hear me. Whatever, you can guess my name too," she told Mac magnanimously.

"Cock blocker?" Mac asked with a grin of recognition.

"You're such a bad boy," the voice chided happily.

Mac shook his head and laughed. Running his hands through his hair he pulled me into a hug.

"It's okay, Zelda. She won't hurt us," he told me.

"You know the cock blocker?"

"Yep."

"Who in the hell is it?" I demanded.

"It's…" he started.

"Nooooooooooooo!" she shouted. "Zelda has to guess or I'll get sucked into a gaping hole and thrown into the carnival from hell featuring twenty-seven of my least favorite former lovers."

"I am so lost I don't know what to do," I mumbled as I put my head in my hands. "That's almost as weird as Chuck's black hole with elevator music."

"Time warp," Mac corrected.

"Whatever," I replied. "It's all just weird."

The gasp of pain and sadness from the voice gave me pause. Did she know Chuck?

"Zelda, you'll have to guess, but it shouldn't be too hard," Mac explained rationally.

"Isn't he adorable," the cock blocking pain in my ass chimed in.

"Yes," I snapped. "Adorable and leaving. Mac, for the Goddess's sake you have to go home. I have to guess who the nut job is, re-evaluate my entire existence, and most likely do an exorcism on said nut job. This is something best handled alone because it could be messy and very profane."

"Not going anywhere," Mac said as he sat back on my bed and got comfortable.

What a douche canoe. If I was sure I wouldn't blow him to Kingdom Come, I smite his superior, sexy, bossy butt right out of the window. Dang it, the list just kept growing—find therapist, learn how to control the redonkulous amount of magic flowing through me, banish the spirit, get laid...

"Can I ask you questions?" I ground out to the spirit.

"Yes you can!"

"Do I know you?" I inquired, still scanning the room for movement. She might not be dangerous, but she still deserved a little ass blasting.

"Biblically, no."

"Mmkay—gross. Are you alive or dead?"

"Debatable," she answered. "I'm here, but it wasn't easy."

"Why in the hell *are* you here?" I snapped. "Who invited you?"

"You did, my dear child," she told me with a giggle.

"You lost me," I said as I pulled on my pigtails.

"Zelda, I received your letter. I received your letter and I came."

My heart pounded in my chest so rapidly, I was sure it was going to pop out. Was this possible? I wrote the letter on a lark. I sent it into the Universe with some magic. I was flabbergasted she actually got it. Maybe my magic wasn't as off as I thought it was.

"Aunt Hildy?" I whispered in shock, awe and fear. Not fear of her, but fear that once she got to know me she'd reject me too... just like my mother had.

Shit. First fucking thing tomorrow I would find a therapist and pay for a year in advance.

"Yes, my beautiful niece. I've come to save the day!"

I fell back on the bed right into Mac's open arms. I pressed my palms to my chest to calm my erratic heartbeat and a small hint of a smile began to pull at my lips.

My life had gone from bizarre to outright freakin' crazy. It was either take the ride or run. Running meant being alone again, but riding meant possible death or the need for more years of therapy than I could afford.

Thinkthinkthink.

I'd never been a weenie and I wouldn't start today. I was going to step up and live my life—my brand new, secretly fabulous and possibly short life.

"Welcome home, Aunt Hildy," I said softly.

"It's lovely to be back. We have a crapload to do! It's going to be so much fun! I can't wait to scare the living hell out of my brother!" she crowed with delight.

I grinned and shook my head.

Let the shit show begin.

Chapter 8

"Holy Goddess in knock-off Zac Posen," Naked Dude shouted as he burst into my bedroom panting like he'd run a marathon.

He was wearing a skintight white sleeveless workout shirt and black yoga pants that looked suspiciously like my black Lululemon yoga leggings. He was barefoot, sweaty and completely freaked out.

"Are you alright?" he demanded as he dropped to his knees and tried to catch his breath.

"Um, are those my yoga pants?" I asked as I wrinkled my nose and pondered if he'd also borrowed a thong.

"Yes, they are your yoga pants," he yelled. "I don't have any yoga pants and I wanted to fit in. I think I fill them out nicely. However, I think I should get a larger size. My left testicle seems to be lodged in my esophagus. I also think I might look better in navy blue."

"Did you run home?" I asked, wondering why he was sweating.

He was a warlock. He could have just poofed in.

"Yessssssss, I ran and it was tremendously unpleasant. I was terrified to use magic considering the amount of out of control power that's floating through the house and evident from at least five miles away," he grunted.

"Seriously?" I asked and wondered if Hildy was still in the room.

"Do you think I would run if it wasn't necessary?" Naked Dude replied wearily. "I also have a message to relay to... what the hell?" he groused as he finally took in my Little Red Riding Hood get-up and Mac's partially clad body on my bed.

"Ummmm..." I muttered trying not to laugh at the look of sheer horror on my father's very handsome face.

"Are you wearing a ten thousand dollar Chanel cape to have illicit relations with a werewolf?" he demanded.

"Holy crap," I gasped out. "This cost ten thousand dollars? Fabdudio, you are so going to end up in the pokey. And let me just tell you, the pokey sucks. I hated every minute of it. My cellmate was certifiable. She made even *me* look sane. Soooo, we have to discuss your shop lifting habits. I mean, I'll keep the cape since I was partially defiled in it, but this shit has got to stop."

"*Oh please,*" Hildy snorted. "*He's richer than Midas. My brother wouldn't steal a candy bar. Of course he's a complete doucheknocker, but he's not a thief.*"

"You're rich?" I asked, shocked.

"Who told you that?" he asked warily.

"Somebody," I replied staring him down.

"That's really neither here nor there," Fabio informed me, completely avoiding my query. "The more important matter at hand is the fact that you should be consorting with warlocks. Not Shifters. You're above him."

"Actually I was beneath him," I shot back. "And you are a fine one to discuss morals."

"You are not supposed to do as I do," Naked Dude snapped. "You're supposed to do as I say."

"Um... Dude, you lost that right before I was born. And you're slowly losing points with each subsequent word that flies from your mouth."

Mac's amused chuckle did not help the situation. Fabio's fingers twitched and I quickly stepped in front of the hot guy on my bed. I was the only one permitted to zap his fine ass.

"Look, you might want to try some reverse psychology. I was on my way to being single again, but you're making me rethink."

"Parenting is hard," Naked Dude whined as he plopped his large frame down in a chair. "I'm not sure I'm doing this very well."

"You're doing fine," I consoled him. "You just have to realize I'm not thirteen."

"*Can we screw with him?*" Hildy begged.

"I don't think it's a good idea right now," I told her.

Naked Dude looked a little pathetic all mussed up and wearing women's yoga pants.

"Who are you talking to?" he barked as he looked around

the room.

"Somebody," I answered cagily.

"That's it. Zelda, you're grounded. The werewolf has to leave and you will stay in your room for the rest of the evening," Fabio announced grandly.

I inhaled deep and blew the air back out slowly. I was this close to magically reducing the size of the yoga pants to extra, extra small, but it might decimate his balls. It would be wrong— even I knew it. I was going to use words not spells.

"Screw with him." I told Hildy. "He's asking for it."

"*Yayayayayayay!*" she squealed. "*He's taking yoga to get limber because he misses licking his balls.*"

"That's disgusting," I said with a shudder. The visual alone activated my gag reflex.

"What's disgusting?" Fabio asked, perplexed.

"I can't believe you're doing yoga just so you can become one with your nads again."

"That's just preposterous," he stuttered not quite able to make eye contact. "I do have a message for…"

"*He slept with the lights on until he was a hundred and fifty,*" Hildy chimed gleefully.

"You're afraid of the dark?" I giggled and watched him squirm.

"I most certainly am not," he huffed.

"*He was obsessed with Dorothy Hamill and wore his hair in the Hamill Wedge for six years,*" she choked out through her laughter. "*I have pictures.*"

"No freakin way." I fell back on the bed and laughed. It was so wrong and so awesome. "You truly sported a wedge cut for six years?"

Fabio froze and his eyes narrowed to slits. Green sparkles burst from his fingertips and began to fly willy nilly around the room.

"*Call him a doucheknocker,*" Hildy said.

"I think we might have screwed with him a bit much," I said as I ducked a rather aggressive blast.

"*Do it! It will be great,*" she insisted.

"I'm supposed to call you a doucheknocker," I mumbled.

"Where is she?" Fabio hissed as he stood and prepared to do some major damage. "Where is my gaping, cavernous, canker sore of a sister? And who in the hell invited her? She can't come back without an invitation—an invitation from an extraordinarily powerful source."

"I guess I did," I admitted, ignoring the part about the powerful source. I'd deal with that nugget later—as in never. "I sent a letter off into the cosmos. She showed up and interrupted my afternoon sex-capades."

"Well, at least the old hag is good for something," Fabio muttered as he reigned in his magic. "Show yourself, you smelly broom flyer."

"I can't, you fart nozzle," Hildy griped, now in full voice for all to hear. "I'm afraid I'll poof away if I try."

"I think you should try," Fabio said with an evil smirk. "I dare you."

"I am not falling for a dare, you testicle slurper," she informed her brother.

"Don't knock it till you try it," he shot back.

Mac and I sat silently and listened to the juvenile name-calling. It was both amusing and disconcerting. Watching two over two hundred year old siblings fighting like they were twelve had not been on my agenda for today.

"Are you guys done?" I asked nicely. "If you're not, you should finish up because I detect in-coming old lady crouch."

"Baba Yaga?" Mac asked as he sat up and pulled on the rest of his clothes.

"Yep. The one and only BabaYopaininmybutt."

"That's terribly rude, darling," Hildy chided. "If Baba hears you say that, she'll zap you bald."

"Then I propose we don't tell her," I said as I quickly made up the bed and tidied the room.

"Aren't you going to change?" Fabio demanded loudly.

"Nope, I'll just button my wildly expensive cape that my questionably rich, ball-obsessed, girly-dressed dad bought me."

"She called me Dad!" Fabio shouted joyously and high-fived the air looking for his sister.

"Oh my Goddess." I rolled my eyes and shook my head. "Did you not hear the rest of the sentence?"

"Nope, just heard *Dad*," he informed me with a huge grin. "Music to my ears."

"He's nuts," I said as I pulled my wild red curls free from the elastics.

"Runs in the family, dear," Hildy volunteered cheerfully.

"Clearly," I mumbled. "Good to know I come by it honestly."

"I love your crazy," Mac whispered in my ear then seated himself in the armchair and waited for the show to commence.

My insides tingled and I had to hold myself back from flinging my body at him. How many guys would have stayed after what we'd just witnessed? He really *did* love my crazy. That was so freakin' hot.

"I heard that," Naked Dude ground out to Mac. "You're very quick with the compliments, young man."

I had to bite down on my lip to stifle my groan. Only my dysfunctional family would think being told that our crazy wasn't offensive amounted to a compliment.

"Zelda," Naked Dude reminded. "I do have to give you a message."

"Hold that thought, Dudio. We have incoming in about five seconds."

The atmosphere in the room changed dramatically. A strong breeze mixed with flecks of sliver and peach glitter blew in short, sharp gusts. The lights flickered and a large mirror ball straight out of a 1980's high school prom appeared on the ceiling. I gasped in dismay. That had better not be permanent. Baba Yaga was eternally trapped in 80's fashion mode. It was funnier to talk about than to witness. Occasionally it gave me hives. The mirror ball worked overtime and we all looked like we were in a disco tech from hell. However, my red cape did look pretty awesome under the lights.

"What a fabulous entrance!" Hildy shouted above the wind whipping violently around and destroying my room. "How I have missed my BFF!"

I held onto the headboard of my bed so I wouldn't get blown out the window and into the front yard. I rolled my eyes and sighed. Of course my nutty dead aunt was best-friends-forever with the certifiable, style-impaired leader of all witches.

Baba Yaga appeared in a blast of colorful smoke, choking and swatting at the idiots who had landed on top of her. Her entrance was usually far more polished than this one. Baba was in fine form on this visit. She rarely travelled without her posse of older than dirt warlocks and today was no exception. However, this time there was a distinct difference. The ten little bobble-headed bastards were chained together and on a leash. Baba Yaga gripped the end of the leash in annoyance and jerked them to attention.

If this was some sick-o sexual thing, I was leaving.

"Surprise!" Baba Yaga trilled as she got to her feet and took a bow.

She looked like a reject from a Duran Duran music video. Baba Yaga was sporting enough hairspray to rip a thousand holes into the ozone layer. For such an exquisitely beautiful woman, her taste was appalling.

"Wonderful!" Hildy squealed. "However, it still can't beat the time you flew in on a fire breathing dragon wearing sequined booty shorts and feathers."

Baba paused and considered.

I held my breath. No one back talked the Yaga. No one.

"Oh my Goddess," Baba Yaga remembered with glee. "I'd forgotten. That was at least a hundred and seventy-five years ago. I was brilliant!"

"Darling, you're still brilliant," Hildy told her lovingly. "The chains are an interesting touch."

"Ahhhhh, Hildy my friend, I've missed you so. And the chains are *not* a touch. They are a necessity. However, I'll get to that in a moment."

Baba Yaga conjured up an iron pole in the center of my bedroom and attached the leash to it. The warlocks shuddered in terror and huddled together. What in hell was going on?

"First things first," Baba muttered as hiked her boob tube up and rubbed her hands together.

Her long beautifully manicured fingers traced patterns in the air and I watched in awe. Small bright blasts of fire danced around her head and shoulders as she closed her eyes and swayed gently to the earth's rhythm. I worried for a brief moment whether the hairspray would go up in flames along with all of us, but figured she had it covered. She was serene, beautiful and a little bit scary. I was watching the MVP of the big leagues. Her voice was clear and loud and I felt it all the way to my toes.

> *"Deep in the darkness there will always be light*
> *Bring to me Goddess, your power so bright*
> *Give the spirit that looms the gift to be seen*
> *For those who adore her, make her sparkle and sheen!"*

In an instant the disembodied voice of my aunt became a floating iridescent figure. She was gorgeous and completely see-through. A silky golden robe danced around her sheer form and her wild red hair flowed around her head.

"Hildy?" Fabio whispered reverently.

"Yes," she answered her brother with a smile and an uplifted middle finger. "I've missed you, you turd knocker."

A lump formed in my throat as I watched them slowly approach each other. Mac took my hand and gently squeezed. His presence grounded me and I held on tight.

Fabio's head tilted to the side and his smile was warm and loving as he flipped his sister the bird. I certainly hoped the habitually rude greeting didn't run in the family too.

"I'm so sorry I wasn't here to defend you," he told her as he reached out to touch her.

"I'm glad you weren't," she said quietly, extending her transparent hand. "It was horrible and I would have been furious if something had happened to you too. One of us has to train our girl."

As their hands passed through each other, Naked Dude stiffened and froze like a block of ice.

"Holy shit," I shouted as I ran to Dude. "What just happened?"

"Well, darn," Baba Yaga muttered. "Didn't know that was a possibility."

Hildy flew frantically around the room as Mac helped me lay my glacial lump of a father on my bed. The warlocks watched with interest until Baba flicked her fingers and blindfolded them all.

"Is he going to be alright?" I demanded. "Should I heal him?"

"I wasn't aware you liked him that much," Baba said as she examined my frigid father. "My goodness, he looks very sexy in these pants."

"Gross and of course I... um... like him. He's my, you know... sperm donor... dad guy," I explained as I felt Dude's neck for a pulse.

"Is that all he is to you?" Baba inquired with interest as she checked out my frozen father's package.

"No, but it's all I can deal with at the moment," I replied as I reached inside myself and pulled on my healing power.

I quickly wrapped Naked Dude in a warm and cozy blanket of magic. The enchantment left my body and made me dizzy and nauseas, but I pushed it through without thought. Shards of ice ran through my veins as I healed him. I shivered and convulsed and prayed to the Goddess. His color slowly came back as he coughed and sputtered. My heart raced as I watched him come to. He needed to stop having near death experiences.

"She called me Dad again," Fabio choked out as he tried to sit up. "You all heard it."

On instinct I smacked him in the head much to the delight of his sister. I was so happy Naked Dude was okay that I got pissed.

"Alright," I yelled, startling everyone in the room including myself. "If I call you Daaaaad, will you stop almost dying all the fucking time?"

The room went silent as did I. Was I really ready to do this? Was I really ready to not do this?

"Daaaaad?" Baba said with a smirk and a giggle. "Are you sure you didn't mean, Dad?"

"Yes. Yes, I'm sure. I meant, Daaaaad," I said as I stared at the ceiling and prayed there was a Shifter therapist in town.

"I'll take it!" Naked Dude yelled. "I'd also like to recommend no one touch Hildy. That hurt like a son of a bitch and I'm fairly sure my balls have shrunk up into my stomach permanently."

"Really sorry," Hildy apologized as she floated close to the ceiling so no one could touch her. "I mean if I knew such a thing was going to happen it would have been far more enjoyable. However, the speed and skill with which you healed your daaaaad was most impressive, Zelda. I couldn't have done better myself."

"Really?" I asked, humbled by her praise.

"Yes. Really."

"Great!" Baba Yaga said as she slapped my daaaaad on the ass. "Now that we have that matter settled… on to the next."

"Which would be?" Mac asked as he stood next to me and put his arm around my still shaking shoulders.

"Is this serious?" Baba asked with a delighted grin as she took in Mac and me.

"No," I said at the same time Mac said, "Yes."

"Wonderful," she said approvingly.

I wasn't sure who she was approving of, but I'd lay money it wasn't me.

"One or several of these shitbombs released the honey badger who killed Hildy," Baba hissed venomously as she referred to the warlocks. They began to keen and wail. "I am too damned tired to deal with this crap. Zelda, I've brought them to you to figure it out and punish the traitor."

"Are you shitting me?" I yelled. She was right out of her gourd.

"Do I look like I'm shitting you?" she demanded.

"Um… not really," I admitted. "But you have the wrong gal for the job. I heal people, not kill them. I'm the Shifter Wanker."

"Yes, well it's all in the semantics," she explained making no sense at all. "Of course you might need some help."

First she tells me to deal with it, and then she tells me I'm not capable of dealing with it. She was clearly off her meds. Why did I even get up this morning?

"My magic is enormous," I snapped.

"Correct," she agreed. "Enormous enough to make the Southern United States a crater. You need to find a witch whose talent lies in blowing up smaller areas… and things. You know, do some damage without taking the entire continent down."

"Why can't you help?" I asked her.

"Because it's not fated to be," Baba explained with a wave of her hand. "This is your territory and you must take care of it."

"Says who?" I shot back. "I don't even know any other witches who like to blow shit up."

"Think hard, my child," Baba said with a raised eyebrow.

"Oh for the Goddess's sake," Daaaaad griped as he glanced down at his ringing cell phone. "I simply cannot communicate with this horrid person anymore. She's been calling for you all day and this time you can deal with her."

"Who are you talking about?" I asked as I realized everyone in the room wanted a piece of me I wasn't willing to give. It was so much easier to just heal the damn Shifters. How had I become the one on charge of the entire shitshow?

"It's someone calling herself Sassy. She says she has your three cats and she's on her way here to dump the mangy, lying, cheating, destructive bastards on your doorstep," Naked Dude said accusingly. "I didn't even know you had other cats. When were you going to tell me?"

"I don't have any other cats," I yelled.

This could not be happening. The thought of my former cellmate Sassy showing up was enough to make me want to blow up the town, cut my losses and run. And cats? I didn't own any cats. I didn't even like cats.

"They're my cats!" Hildy clapped her hands in joy. "I've been wondering where they'd gone."

"Why does this Sassy person have your cats?" Mac asked Hildy.

"Do you believe in fate, my dear pretty boy?" Baba Yaga asked him.

"I do," he replied evenly.

"Then hold on because fate will be here in about an hour," she replied with a laugh that made my stomach churn.

Sassy liked to blow shit up. Sassy also made me want to remove my own head with a dull butter knife. She was on her way to my home with my inherited pets and there was probably very little I could do to stop the certifiable freak from hell.

I inhaled deeply and prayed to the Goddess for strength.

I could do this. I had to do this.

What was the worst thing that could happen?

Shitshitshitshitshit.

Chapter 9

Sassy was just as pretty as I remembered—all perky boobs, perky butt and blonde hair. However, she was twice as insane.

"They've been arrested by animal control six times in the last week alone for disorderly conduct," Sassy griped in her outdoor voice, pacing my living room in agitation as magical sparks flew off of her like static electricity. "The smelly bastards have eaten me out of house and home, and started a gambling ring for familiars. No matter what I did they wouldn't leave so I threw them in the car and brought them back."

"Why didn't you just zap them here?" I asked as I took in the three fat felines sitting on my couch attending to their privates.

"You think I didn't try?" she screeched. "They're evil minions of Satan. It was impossible. Every time I zapped them the magic came back on me tenfold. You should see my ass."

She went to pull down her pants and I screamed.

"No! I will not look at your butt. Nine months in the pokey with you and your ass was enough. I refuse to have your naked backside burned into my brain," I said with my hands raised ready to conjure a permanent set of pants on her if she tried to remove them. "And how in the hell did you figure out they were mine... not to mention where I was living?"

"Well," she informed me smugly. "Along with my talent for fornication and explosives, I've discovered I can dig into jackass's brains and extract info. The little fuckers sang like birds once I dove in and scrambled their teeny, tiny bits of gray matter."

"That sucked," the cat in the middle of the trio announced in a voice that belonged on a cartoon gangster.

"I found it arousing," the one on the right said, sounding like Johnny Cash with a head cold.

I stared at the group and sighed. What harm were three more mangy cats in the myriad of crap that kept piling up? Clearly they overate. I'd never seen such obese cats in my life—especially the one in the middle.

Being alone with Sassy was challenging. The rest of the group had disappeared at my request before she'd arrived, except Mac. He'd refused. He promised to stay out of sight unless I needed him, or he felt I needed him. Baba Yaga had taken Daaaaad and Hildy off to Goddess knows where for some fun and the turdball warlocks were unhappily incarcerated in my basement.

My plan was to deal with Sassy and get rid of her. Then I was going to deal with the warlocks in the basement and get rid of them. And then I would finally deal with the lurking fucking evil and get rid of it. If I was still alive when I finished, I was going to go get my red cape and get laid. It was a fine plan—sadly much easier said than done.

"Names?" I demanded of the menagerie on the sofa.

"I'm Fat Bastard," the gray one with the white tummy in the middle grunted. "Jango Fett is the randy son of a bitch on my right and Boba Fett is the deadly fucker on my left."

"I will dazzle you with my razzamatazz," Jango Fett, a calico with a double chin, told me with a leer and a wink.

"Lovely," I muttered with an eye roll. "And you three sorry excuses for cats belonged to my Aunt Hildy?"

"That's right, Dollface. And you best watch it with the trash talk or I'll jerk a kink in your bahookey," Boba Fett, a white cat with gray splotches informed me.

"Interesting," I said as I sat down on my hands. I was not going to run the risk of inadvertently zapping the little shit and getting it shot right back at me.

"You see?" Sassy snarled. "They're heinous."

"And you're hot," Fat Bastard told Sassy. "And you're not so bad yourself," he added to me with a wink and a crude kitty hip thrust.

"I'd bet it takes you about thirty minutes to get there," Jango said with a sly grin. "I could get you there in ten."

"Get me where?" I asked not really wanting the answer.

"To the big O," he said smarmily.

All three little idiots high fived with their kitty paws and then went right back to getting down on their nads.

"Alrighty, you have almost rendered me speechless. Almost…The three of you are on probation. I'm pretty sure this will not be your forever home considering I'm feeling the need to run you over with my car. Repeatedly."

"Don't think she won't do it," Sassy threatened them gleefully. "She killed her last familiar and spent nine months in the pokey for it. She's fucking crazy."

"Impressive," Fat Bastard congratulated me. "What are you? A wise guy?"

"Nope, just an unstable, out of control witch who's not fond of cats," I replied.

"I can make you an offer you can't refuse," Boba Fett told me with narrowed eyes as he took a brief break from cleansing his testes.

"What the hell are you talking about?" I snapped.

I did not have time for this. I had warlocks in my basement, my family was on the lose somewhere in the community, the fucking evil was still lurking, and Sassy the Heinous was standing in my living room.

"Don't underestimate him," Fat Bastard warned in a muffled voice with his head buried in his crotch.

"No worries," I assured him. "I never underestimate stupidity."

"Thank you," Boba said.

"Welcome," I replied with a shake of my head.

What was I going to do with them and Sassy? I didn't want them here. They were rude, crude and disgusting. As I pondered the fresh hell I was in, Sassy let loose.

"Are you wearing Prada?" she asked with an unpleasant look on her face.

"I am," I replied carefully. One never knew where the conversation was headed with Sassy the Unstable.

"How is it you're wearing Prada and I'm wearing Gap?"

"Well, let's see," I hissed as little icy blue sparks of pissed off-ness flew from my fingers and began to hop around the room. "My cat that I killed wasn't really dead. Turns out he's my father and he's loaded. How? No clue, but I'm quite sure it's shady. He enjoys buying slash stealing me shit and I have ceased to argue the point. He has outstanding taste. However, the down side is he's getting limber so he can lick his gonads again. I popped about forty rubbery evil honey badgers to death and healed about as many Shifters. It hurts like hell to do it, but it's my new job. My title is Shifter Whisperer, but I prefer Shifter Wanker. If you laugh I will permanently seal your lips shut."

I took a huge breath and realized I wasn't quite done yet.

The bewildered looks on the faces of my audience did little to deter me. I was on a fucking roll.

"My aunt came back as a ghost while I was trying to get laid dressed up as Little Red Riding Hood plus a wolf who has a kangaroo son named Jeeves thinks I'm his mate. I was passed out for two weeks and now I have probably about three days left max on my life because of some lurking fucking evil. Roger the rabbit is addicted to porn and Chuck the bear is trying to kill himself in my tree. I have too much magic and I don't know how to control it. I'm probably going to wipe the United States off the map by accident. Not to mention, I have Baba Yomamma's traitorous warlocks locked up in my basement which she informs me I now have to deal with and punish. And apparently I'm stuck in Assjacket, West Virginia. They don't even have a Target in this hellhole. If *that* doesn't merit me getting to wear some fucking Prada, then I don't know what does."

"Um... okay," Sassy mumbled as she tried to process the diatribe I'd just spouted.

"That's hot," Fat Bastard said as his cohorts nodded in agreement.

I took another deep cleansing breath and made some decisions. At this point I didn't care if they were good decisions. I just wanted to move forward—preferably without Sassy in my line of vision or within three hundred miles.

"Sassy, I'd say thank you for bringing me the ball sack obsessed felines, but since I'm not even remotely thankful, I'll just grin and bear it," I told her with a smile that resembled a wince. "I'm sorry you had to drive the bastards all the way here, but you're free to go. Far. Far, far away and it would also be good if you could forget my address."

Sassy stood still in the middle of the room, wrung her hands and began to cry.

Shitballs. Could this day get any worse?

"I don't have anywhere to go. Those little fat fuckers got me kicked out of town. Permanently," she blubbered.

My stomach roiled and my vision blurred. This was not happening.

"Mmmkay," I choked out. "You can try a new town. You must have some friends somewhere who would love to see you."

"I don't have any friends," she sobbed. "Only you."

"Oh my Goddess, I don't even like you," I yelled.

"I don't like you either," she shouted back. "But you're all I have left in this world, Zelda."

"Who did I screw over to get into this situation?" I grumbled.

"Don't know, but I'd be happy to oblige," Jango Fett offered.

"You." I pointed at Jango. "Zip it now or we're going to the driveway to see how many lives you have left."

"Roger that," Jango said.

"This is a big house," Sassy reasoned through her hysterics. "I can live with you."

"Hell to the no," I said as I closed my eyes and tried to avoid the train wreck that was my life. "Where were you before you came here and what was your mission?"

"I was in Butthole, Kentucky, and I have no clue what the hell my mission was supposed to be. I got to a house Baba Yaga gave me an address for and the dumbass cats were there. I've been hanging on by a thread for weeks."

"Was the town really called Butthole?" I asked.

"No. Is the name of this town really Assjacket?"

"No, but it fits."

"Same with Butthole."

I was appalled to realize Sassy's crazy might be similar to mine.

"So you've just been taking care of cats for a month?" I asked shocked and pissed.

What kind of mission was that? I'd almost died several times in the last few weeks. Why had Sassy gotten off so easy?

"I'd hardly describe blowing up half of Butthole, seducing three fourths the male population in the town, and trying to kill us on a daily basis taking care of us," Fat Bastard muttered as he gagged and prepared to heave up a hairball on my couch.

"You puke, you eat," I informed him.

He swallowed back his gift and gave me a furry thumbs up.

"Wait. You blew up the town?" I asked Sassy with raised brows.

"I didn't mean to," she snapped. "The damn cats kept standing in front of buildings when I was aiming at them."

"You're a fucking menace," I said as I began to pace the room.

"Your point?" Sassy shot back.

"You're a slutty, destructive, brain picking mess," I said.

"Again, I ask—your point?"

"Oh my Goddess," I grumbled as I shoved the cats over and flopped down on the couch. "As much as I'm pretending to not like Assjacket in fear of losing my reputation as someone who doesn't care, I really don't want to run the risk of you destroying it."

"What if I promise not to blow anything up?" she bargained.

The cats snickered in disbelief and I had to agree. I sat

silently and waited for her to continue because I knew she would.

"Um... I won't seduce more than three men and um..."

I put my hands over my eyes until I realized Jango had his paw on my left boob.

"Move it or lose it," I hissed.

He quickly withdrew his soon to be stump as Sassy kept going.

"I promise to help around the house unless it requires actual cleaning. I promise not to borrow your clothes without asking unless you say no or you're not here and I need to look good. I promise to continue to try to kill the cats but only in large fields without buildings. I promise to put the toilet seat down and I..."

"You pee with the toilet seat up?" I asked perplexed by that one.

"No, but I'm trying to impress you," she explained.

"Not working."

Sassy began to glow. I did not take this as a good sign and neither did the cats. They dove under the couch. Well, they tried. Their enormous asses didn't fit and were hanging out.

"Sassy?"

"Yes?"

"Are you about to blow up my house?" I inquired as casually as I could.

"Um... no?"

"Good answer." I heaved a sigh as the glowing subsided. "You have five seconds to give me a solid enough reason for you to stay. Unless you can convince me, you have to leave."

"You didn't like any of my suggestions so far?" she whined.

"Nope."

Sassy pulled on her wild blond hair and bit down on her lip as she thought. I considered taking her out to the yard for fear she would blow up the house when I told her she had to go. There was no answer in this world good enough for me to let her stay.

"You said you have lurking fucking evil?" she asked slowly.

"Yes."

"You have Baba Yasshole's warlocks in the basement?"

"Yes."

"Are they involved?"

"You mean are they dating anyone?" I groaned and rolled my eyes.

"Gross," she shouted. "I have higher standards than that. I meant are they involved with the evil?"

"Possibly."

"You have a Little Red Riding Hood costume?"

"What the hell does that have to do with anything?" I demanded.

"Nothing," she assured me. "I just think it's cool."

"Thank you."

"Welcome."

"You have too much magic?" Sassy continued her questions.

"Yes."

"You need me," she said with a satisfied smirk.

"Not following."

"It's simple. I think this is my mission. I can do things you can't."

"Still not following."

"Baba Yoyo obviously gave me your heinous fucking cats for a reason. I can blow shit up for you including the warlock wankers in the basement. If your magic is out of control, you tell me what to do and I'll do it. I can dive into the brains of anyone you want me to and get the truth. We'll use the cats as a shield and anything that tries to harm us will get it right back at them in a way that will leave scars. My ass can attest to this."

Shitmotherhumper. She was making sense.

"Please Zelda?" she begged. "It'll be fun."

"Fun is not the word that comes to mind," I said warily.

I stood up and paced again. I knew I needed help.

Had fate made me hold off until Sassy came back into my life?

Could I run the risk of letting her loose on a town that I was secretly coming to love? Could I run the risk of not letting her loose?

"If I take you to the basement can you get inside the heads of the warlocks and figure out which one is the traitor?" I asked already knowing I was going to let her stay.

"Um... yes?"

"That didn't sound too positive," I said as I stopped pacing and got in her face.

"I'm sure I can," she promised quickly. "I've only been inside cat's heads, but how different can a warlock be?"

"Extremely different," Fat Bastard grunted from under the couch.

"Whatever," Sassy snapped. "A male brain is a male brain. They're all tiny and obsessed with tits. I can do this."

"She's got a point," Boba said as he unwedged himself. "We also think about..."

"Stop," I cut him off. "I do not want to hear what else you think about. I have a very active gag reflex. It will make me smite you and I'm not in the mood for a ricochet smitation. We clear?"

"Yes. Yes we are," Boba said. "However, I'd like to go on record as saying you have tremendous knockers."

"That's it. I've had enough," Mac ground out as he strode into the room and right over to the cats. "One more sexual innuendo to my woman and I remove the balls you seem to be so fond of."

"Easy there, buddy," Fat Bastard said as he covered his jewels. "We was just joking with your girl."

"Oh my Goddess," Sassy gasped. "Is that your wolf?"

"He is *not* my wolf, but if you touch him I will remove your hands. If you look at him I will gouge out your eyeballs," I hissed and then smacked myself in the head.

"Yes, I'm her wolf," Mac said with a very self-satisfied grin and a bow. "And she's my witch."

"That's hot," Fat Bastard said and punctuated it by grabbing his kitty nads.

Sassy nodded in agreement.

"One more word out of any of you and you will lose the ability to speak for a very long time," I warned. "I am quite sure I have made some monumental mistakes in the last five minutes, but I'm going to go with it. We are going to take a field trip to the basement and hopefully live through it. This is not a democracy. It's a clusterfuck waiting to happen. I am the freakin' boss so whatever stupid decision I make we will all comply with. And no back talk. Got it?"

Everyone nodded silently. Mac winked. The cats saluted and Sassy flipped me off.

Everything was as it should be.

I smiled.

I still had it. *What* I had, I wasn't exactly sure... but I definitely still had it.

Chapter 10

"Holy shit, they're ugly," Sassy muttered as we all took in the warlocks.

The mini magicmen were huddled together inside of a large metal cage. Cots, pillows and blankets were available to them, but they had ignored the provided comforts. The warlocks congregated in the center and swayed menacingly. Sassy was correct. They were ugly—and angry. Their small older-than-dirt bodies trembled with fury. It was unnerving. Even the cats were uncomfortable and strangely quiet.

The basement of my new home happened to be filled with cages. When I'd first arrived it had been a mystery to me. Turns out it was a hospital of sorts for the Shifters. The cages were for their safety while injured. I didn't particularly like them, but the Shifters didn't seem to mind.

However, the warlocks didn't seem to be enjoying them at all.

"So what do you do to get inside their heads?" I asked Sassy as I nervously watched the warlocks watching us.

"Well, um…" she started hesitantly.

"You don't have a clue, do you?" I hissed.

Damn it, I should have made her leave when I'd had the chance. This had disaster written all over it. I could always just ask the bastards which one had let the honey badger go. I had nothing to lose. It might even work.

"Can they use magic?" Mac asked as he removed his shirt and went for his pants.

"The chains should preclude them from it or at the very

least dull their power," I said as I gaped at him. This was not the time or the place to have a quickie. "What exactly are you doing?"

"I'm going to shift," he informed me with a knowing grin. "I'll be better able to protect you."

"Right," I said as the heat moved swiftly up my neck and landed on my face. "I knew that."

"Like you knew number seven?" he asked.

"Exactly like I knew number seven," I answered with a giggle.

"Do you have an eight pack?" Sassy asked Mac breathlessly.

"Do you value your eyesight?" I snapped at the swooning Sassy as I stepped in front of a partially naked Mac.

"Yep," she replied quickly and lowered her eyes. "But that is one impressive stomach. You're really lucky."

"I have a three pack," Fat Bastard volunteered.

"Where?" Sassy asked.

"Under my love padding," he told her without cracking a smile.

"Enough," I snapped. "We have stuff to do. You either can or can't get into their minds. Which is it?"

"I can," she said with more confidence than sense. "I can and I will. Didn't you say your wolf had a son?"

"I did," I replied and bit back my laugh.

"Is he available?" she inquired.

I glanced over at Mac who shrugged and chuckled. Picturing Jeeves and Sassy together was absolutely wrong on every level.

"Yes. Yes, he's available. But first we have to make it out of the basement alive in order for you to hit on him."

"I'm on it," Sassy said now far more determined than she had been just moments ago.

She was such a hooker.

"All right you itty bitty little sons of bitches," she shouted. "I'm about to blow your minds."

"Wait. You're not really going to blow up their minds," I whispered frantically as I grabbed Sassy's arm.

"I sure as fuck hope not," she whispered back. "That would be a damn mess."

"You will do no such thing," the meanest looking warlock in the front bellowed. "I forbid it."

"You're not in any kind of position to be giving orders here, little dude," I said as I stepped toward the cage.

Mac was right with me in his wolf form. His large body was pressed against mine. The cats stood between Mac's front paws and Sassy flanked my other side. The warlocks glared and gnashed their teeth.

"*You're* the powerful one?" The small man laughed derisively and the rest of the tiny turds joined him.

"Never underestimate the power of stupidity," Boba Fett reminded me.

"Where did you hear that?" I asked while keeping my eyes trained on the warlocks.

"Some really smart, wildly unstable, cat hating witch said it to me recently," he replied.

"Must have been a brilliant witch," I said.

"That remains to be seen," Boba shot back with a smirk.

It certainly did.

"Alright, I'm going to give you douchewanks a chance to do this the easy way," I nicely explained to the angry mob in the cage. "You can tell me which one of you idiots let the honey badger go and the rest of you can go home to your caves. Or we can do it the hard, untested and somewhat dangerous way."

"And that would be?" one of the warlocks snarled.

Goddess, they were a nasty bunch.

"That would be a mind meld, brain freeze, info gathering cluster-humper of a first time try on something other than a cat," Sassy informed them as she cracked her knuckles and adjusted her ample bosom.

"Oh hell no," a warlock mumbled.

"That's right, assmonkeys." I backed up my former foe with force, and a confidence I was far from feeling. "Start talking or Sassy will go ape shit on your brain matter."

"This is ridiculous," the one in the front said as he raised his hands in the air and narrowed his gaze at us.

"Put your hands down. Now," I warned as I raised my own. "I don't want to hurt you."

"Like you could hurt us," he growled and raised his hands higher.

"Duck," Fat Bastard shouted as a massive and violent streak of magenta magic left the warlocks' hands and flew at our group.

So much for their magic being muted...

Mac shoved Sassy and me behind him and the cats—well, they freakin' blew my mind.

It felt like slow motion, but it was fast and it was vicious. Fat Bastard hopped up and planted his back kitty feet in second position and raised his front paws in the air. Jango Fett back-flipped on to Fat Bastard's outstretched paws and Boba climbed to the top of the furry pyramid. The fat furry felines now stood piled high about six feet tall and were hissing and screeching like a deflating hot air balloon.

The magic bolt hit Jango square in the chest and I screamed. Burning cat fur singed my nose and brought tears to my eyes. I prayed to the Goddess I could heal him when this ended. I didn't really like him and his grabby paws much, but he'd just taken one for the team.

Boba leaned forward and ingested the sparks from the massive fiery zap and belched loudly. The warlocks watched in fascinated shock as Fat Bastard reached up and set his own paws on fire with the singed fur of Jango who stood atop him.

I was going to have a shit ton of healing to do if this is what the dorky cats did for fun... however, they'd only just begun.

"Fire," Fat Bastard ordered.

"Oh shit, get low," Sassy cried out as she pulled me to the floor next to her. "This is about to get ugly."

She was correct.

All three cats contorted in ways their girth should have prohibited them from moving. It was almost balletic... if you could call what the fat furballs did ballet. The magenta blast they'd taken in grew in size at least ten times as it whirled and swirled around them. They laughed maniacally as the warlocks blanched and tried to back up.

"Shoot the fuckers!" Boba grunted as he coughed up the magic he'd eaten like a hairball from hell.

The enormous flaming streak flew right back at the warlock who'd sent it and he screamed in agony as it zapped the hell out of him and his cronies. The hopping, wailing and swearing was almost funny, but I was unsure if they were just damaged or burning to death.

"Oh my Goddess, are they dying?" I asked Sassy as I tried to make out what was happening through the billowing smoke.

"Not real sure," she admitted with a shudder as the screaming increased. "We can't exactly get info out of dead guys."

"That is probably the smartest thing you've ever said," I told her.

"Really?" she asked, delighted.

"Yes. Really."

I stood up and raised one hand to the sky. I held my nose with the other as I was terrified I'd throw up due to the stench. Puking in the middle of a spell was sure to result in something very very bad.

"Goddess on high, come to my aid

Stop the destruction the good cats have made
Spare the un-tried, withdraw the last hit
Help me deal with these warlocks even though they are... um...
shit"

Waving my hand I let a soothing lavender haze leave my body. The billowing smoke and orange flames receded quickly and the stench of burning flesh and hair disappeared. Thankfully my cats were fine. They needed a bath but they were alive and quite pleased with themselves. The warlocks on the other hand hadn't fared nearly as well, but they weren't dead and crispy. I shuddered at the thought of what that blast would have done to us if the cats hadn't been here.

Mac, still in his wolf form, growled menacingly at the shocked and injured warlocks. Sassy gathered the cats close.

"You little shits were amazing," she cooed as she patted out some still smoking fur on Boba Fett. "Your magic is far more enjoyable when it's not aimed at my ass.

"Interesting spell," Fat Bastard commented as he preened under Sassy's attention.

"Shut the fuck up, I was under pressure," I informed him defensively. Even I was surprised I'd used an expletive in my magic. "It worked didn't it?"

"It did," he conceded with grin.

"You're evil," the smoking warlock in the front cried out as he smacked at his still smoldering clothes.

"Pot, kettle, black," I shot back. "I certainly hope you little jerks have learned a lesson here. My cats can kick your ass. No more funny stuff or I let you fry. We clear?"

"You're keeping us?" Boba Fett inquired hopefully.

"Um... yes," I said as I dropped my chin to my chest.

Mac turned and gave me a funny look, but I just shrugged and rolled my eyes. What was I supposed to do? They'd saved our lives. The old Zelda would have said thank you grudgingly and then kicked the disgusting bastards out. The new Zelda couldn't do that. I wasn't sure if I liked the new Zelda, but she wasn't giving me much of a choice.

Need damn therapist. Yesterday.

"I'm keeping you for now, but all three of you are on probation," I warned. "You touch my boobs or butt, we're going to the driveway to test my backing-over-cat skills."

"Roger that," Jango said happily as he patted down his privates for burning embers. "What about side boob?"

I gave him a glare which zipped his kitty lips. Mac punctuated my warning with a growl.

"So boss-lady, what do you wanna do here?" Sassy asked as she stood up and examined the warlocks.

"You want to try your unskilled hand at interrogation?" I asked her.

"Yes. Yes I do. Let me keep the cats down here with me and I'll be fine," she said. "Give me two hours and I'll have your bad guy. And I swear if I blow one up, it will be an accident."

"Good enough for me," I said as the warlocks squeaked in fear. "I'd suggest you refrain from throwing any more zingers," I advised the little magic turds. "My cats will shoot it right back and I won't be down here to save your mean little asses. Capisce?"

"Excellent choice of word," Jango complimented me. "I use it daily."

"Thank you."

"Welcome, Dollface."

"Sassy, you will be careful. I don't like you, but you're beginning to grow on me like a slightly irritating fungus. I also like my house and want it to stay in one piece."

"I promise to do my best," she vowed.

Her words didn't calm my fluttering stomach, but it would have to do for the moment. I needed to have a few words with Baba Yaga and then I wanted a brief town meeting to get all my people up to speed. If I worked fast and efficiently I could still get laid before sundown.

My plans were set.

"Hang on, I have to do one more thing," I said as I raised my hands up and took a deep breath. I wasn't entirely comfortable leaving Sassy and my vile new pets down in the basement alone with no protection.

"Goddess of mine, hear my call
Bind the magic shits so my friends will not fall
For those that are true, may their power come back
But for he who is not, make him a magic-less hack"

"Another interesting spell," Fat Bastard commented. "I like it."

"The swearing is a nice touch," Sassy added approvingly.

"Well, I'm kind of finding my mojo here," I admitted. "I figure I need my own style."

"You got it cornered, Sweetcheeks," Boba Fett congratulated me.

"Thank you. Mac, come with me. We have work to do and then I have to tell you a story."

The cats and Sassy snickered. Mac quickly shifted back to human form and I dressed him with a flick of my hand before Sassy's eyeballs popped out of her head.

Mac's over-confident grin annoyed me and turned me on. I was becoming as possessive about him as he was about me. Yet another reason for therapy. It was the one thing I was determined to find out during the town meeting.

I was going to take care of my freakin' mental health if it was the last thing I did.

Chapter 11

"Is this a fucking joke?" I demanded to the group of confused Shifters. I stomped my foot and hurled blast of magic at the same tree Chuck had tried to hang himself in this morning blowing a branch off.

My front yard was filled with Shifters milling about as I threw a hissy fit on the lawn. The raccoon Shifters, Wanda and her adorable four year old son Bo were handing out refreshments, and my buddies, Simon the skunk and Deedee the deer were putting out folding chairs for the large group which had formed.

"No sweetie," Wanda said as she offered me lemonade and a cookie. "Roger the rabbit is a wonderful therapist. He's helped many of us."

"He's the town gossip and he has… um… issues," I said as I remembered I'd promised not to share Roger's porno addiction. "There has to be another therapist in town."

"Nope," Simon cut in. "He's the only one. He helped me get over my fear of the dark. It was a great relief to the entire community when I got cured."

"Why was the town concerned about your being afraid of the dark?" I asked as I pilfered a second cookie from the tray Wanda was holding.

"Because his stinker trigger is connected to his fear level," Wanda gently explained as not to embarrass Simon.

"She's correct," Simon added with a blush and a chuckle. "It was awfully smelly at night for about ten years before Roger helped me put a plug in it—so to speak."

This could not be happening. There was no way in hell I was going to be doctored by Roger the butt plug wielding boob ogler.

"I'll just go to another town to get my head shrunk," I told them.

"You'll have to go to another state for someone who can deal with magical beings," Simon said as he helped an older mountain lion Shifter to a seat. "The closest one I know of is in Florida."

"Maybe there's a witch around here who can take me on," I muttered as I searched the crowd for Daaaaad, Hildy and Baba Yaga. Where in the hell were they?

"Interesting you say that," Simon said thoughtfully. "I've detected the presence of another witch in the area."

"Well, there *is* kind of another witch in the area," I admitted and wondered if Hildy wanted her presence known.

"Really?" Wanda asked concerned. "Is she after your job?"

"Absolutely not," I assured her and Simon. "She's a good witch. Oh and my cellmate, Sassy from the pokey is here for a visit—hopefully a very short one. But neither of those witches want my job."

"Good," Simon said with relief. "Witch showdowns are quite frightening."

"Buttbomb explosion frightening?" I asked with a smirk.

"Yep, big ones," he replied with a laugh. "Should we get started here?"

"We should," I told Simon as we walked to the front of the crowd.

"Is there a reason we're meeting outside?" he asked as he gestured for all to take a seat.

"Sassy the Shitastic is in the basement digging info out of Baba Yaga's warlock's brains. One of the little assmonkeys let the honey badger go free. There's a fine chance I won't have a house in the next hour, so I figured we'd be safer in the yard."

"Good thinking," Simon casually congratulated me as if I'd told him I'd eaten all my veggies. "However the witch I sensed…"

A gardenia scented wind blew up from out of nowhere and hundreds of tiny teal and hot pink birds zipped in and out of the crowd. Silver and gold glitter rained down and I rolled my eyes.

The Shifters danced around and waved at me with joy.

"It's not me," I yelled above the chatter, but no one heard or they just didn't care. Goddess, was this how she always made her entrances? I was clearly slacking.

"I'm baaaaaaaaaack!" Hildy squealed to a shocked and

delighted crowd as she floated above making sure she was out of touching range.

"Hold that thought Simon," I said as I shook my head at my Aunt's over the top entrance.

My Daaaaaad stood below her, grinning like an idiot. Thankfully he was no longer sporting my yoga pants. He was in jeans and a nice button down shirt.

"It's Hildy," Deedee shouted with glee. "And she's transparent!"

"I'm a ghost!" she explained to the excited yet wary Shifters.

"Are you here to stay?" Little Bo asked as he reached up to touch her.

"No touching," Daaaaad said as he gently pushed Bo's hands down. "She'll freeze your ass off."

"He's right," Hildy said sadly. "You can look but not touch."

"Oh my Goddess." Wanda dropped the tray of cookies and paled. "Does Chuck know?"

"Does Chuck know what?" I asked as I searched the crowd for him.

I didn't see him and worried for a brief second he might be hanging in a tree, but he had promised Mac he wouldn't off himself until the danger had passed.

"I don't know how long I can stay," Hildy told the rapt group. "But we will make the most of my visit while I'm here."

Hildy scanned the crowd as she flew above. Her smile turned to a frown as if she couldn't find what she was searching for.

"Not everyone is here," she said with a pout.

"I'm pretty sure they are," I replied.

"No. Someone is missing," she insisted as she flew frantically around the excited crowd.

"She's talking about Chuck," Wanda whispered in my ear.

"Why is she looking for Chuck?" I whispered back.

"Because she loves him."

"Hildy and Chuck?" I asked.

"Sitting in a tree. K I S S I N G," Simon said. "He was distraught for weeks after she died."

"He's still distraught," I told him. "He tried to hang himself in my tree."

"Oh dear, that won't work out like he thinks it will," Wanda said as she shook her head sadly.

"You can't be sure about that," Simon countered.

"Confused here," I muttered.

"He wants to be with Hildy," Wanda explained.

"She's dead," I stated the obvious.

"Exactly," Simon said.

"Oh my Goddess," I gasped out. "He's trying to kill himself to be with her?"

The Shifters went silent as a huge roar and an enormous black bear burst from the tree line and bound into the middle of the chaos. Hildy flew higher as Chuck, in his bear form, reached for her.

"No," she shouted. "You can't touch me. I'll hurt you."

He jumped and growled, but to no avail. Hildy flew higher.

"No. Chuck, you cannot touch me. I will not allow it," she said in a voice filled with anguish.

Chuck's agonized wail made my heart hurt. Silver tears streamed from my beautiful aunt's eyes. Chuck fell to the ground and beat the dirt. The Shifters backed up respectfully and gave him room. My heartbroken friend clawed at his fur and banged his huge head against the hard ground.

"Chuck stop," Hildy cried. "You'll hurt yourself, my love."

Hildy tried to stop him with magic, but to her shock and dismay her magic didn't work. For a brief moment, I wondered if it was because she was a ghost... then the reality hit. My stomach churned. Her magic didn't work because I had her magic inside me. I'd taken it back from the honey badger who had stolen it from her when he killed her. I was the walking talking magical menace. Not only did I have Hildy's power... I also had my own.

Damndamndamn.

Chuck ignored my Aunt's impassioned plea and the Shifters—being idiot Shifters, joined him. They all fell to the ground and began banging their heads and clawing at their bodies.

No. Fucking. Way.

The was no way in hell I was going to heal forty Shifters with self-inflicted head wounds because they felt some kind of bizarre need to further Chuck's cause. Thankfully Simon, Wanda, Bo, Daaaaad and Mac had not joined the kool-aid drinking dumbasses.

"Enough," I shouted and flung my hands in the air. I knew I was taking a risk using my power on a large group, but they'd given me no choice. If I had to heal all of them, I'd be passed out for weeks. I didn't have time for it. I had obese new pets, a heinous and potentially highly explosive houseguest, some evil to banish, and an x-rated fairy tale to finish.

Sparkling rainbow colored flames shot from my fingertips and all forty or so Shifters levitated into the air and hung there like helium balloons. Their befuddled faces almost made me laugh. However, I was terrified to let them down. There was no telling what would occur.

"Whoops, didn't know that would happen," I mumbled as I stared at my hands.

"You didn't plan that?" Daaaaad asked with concern.

"Not exactly. I just wanted them to stop banging their heads on the ground. That would give me the mother of all migraines to heal that shit," I said in my defense.

"Goddess," Daaaaad said as he ran his hands through his hair in worried agitation. "We need to get you trained. Pronto."

"Ya think?" I snapped. "At least I didn't blow up the countryside."

"I think what you did was outstanding," Mac said as he took in the spectacle with pride.

"You just want in my pants," I told him.

"Correct, but I still think you did the right thing," he said with a grin.

Daaaaad shook his head and groaned as he gave Mac the stink eye. "You know I can ground you, young lady."

"You know I can shrink all your boxer briefs, Daaaaad—while you're wearing them."

"You wouldn't," he huffed as his hands went instinctively to his man jewels.

"Try me," I countered.

"Remind me never to get on your bad side," Mac said.

I rolled my eyes and laughed. "I promise never to damage your Bon Jovi."

"Jon Bon Jovi is here?" Simon asked as he scanned the hovering Shifters.

"Shit," I muttered and I gave Mac a lopsided apologetic smile. "Guess I don't have to worry about Roger letting the rock star out of your pants."

"No," Mac said with a huge sigh and a chuckle. "You did just fine on your own."

"Oooohhhhhhh, I get it," Simon said with a thumbs up. "I call mine The Hulk."

"TMI, Simon," I told my skunk buddy as all the male Shifters began shouting out the names of their man rods.

What had I started?

"Okay," I yelled. "That's quite enough. I'm delighted and repulsed that you've all named your packages, but I have enough nightmares as it is."

"I call mine John Holmes," Roger the rabbit therapist shouted in the silence.

There was simply no way in hell I was going to him for my

problems. Not gonna happen.

"Mmkay, while that's all kinds of awesome, beyond gross and massive wishful thinking, we have business to attend to and the next Shifter who shares his weenie's name shall lose said weenie."

The silence was so thick it could be cut with a knife. I suppressed my giggle and forged on. Glancing around, I realized someone else was missing. Not good—not good at all.

"Where is Baba Yomamma?" I asked Daaaaad and Hildy.

"She left," Hildy said as she floated as near to Chuck as she dared.

"What do you mean she left?" I demanded. "Her freakin' warlocks are in my basement being put through the ringer by Sassy the Terminator. Baba Yagahumper can't leave those creepy doucheholes here."

"Well, she did. But she'll be back next Tuesday. We have a date," Daaaaad informed me as he strutted back and forth like a peacock.

Oh. My. Hell. Daaaaad and Baba Yogibooboo? What was the world coming to?

"Back the fuck up," I groused. "You cannot date Baba Yaga."

"Clearly I have no say about your dating life," Daaaaad snipped as he gave Mac a pissy look. "So therefore my sex-capades are off limits to you."

"Shitballs. You've just put an un-erasable image in my head," I squealed in horror.

"Roger the rabbit can probably help you with that," Hildy chimed in.

"No. No, he probably can't," I disagreed. I barely swallowed back my need to scream that Roger was more than likely too busy whacking off to porn to actually be a therapist. He'd named his peenie John Holmes.

"Anyhoo," Daaaaad went on. "Baba had to leave. She felt quite sure you could handle things."

"Does it really look like I can handle things?" I queried sarcastically as I gestured to my dangling neighbors.

"You're doing fine, dear," Hildy said without a whole lot of oomph behind it.

"Yeah, that's debatable," I said, and then turned to my daaaad. "And I will never call Baba Yostuckintheeighties, 'Mom'."

"You were never going to call me Dad," he informed me smugly.

"I am so close to going back to Naked Dude I can taste it," I warned.

Daaaaad made the international zip the lip motion and backed up. Clearly he wasn't going to risk the moniker change. Smart move.

"Okay..." I got back to the reason I'd called everyone here. "Here's the deal. One of Baba Yaga's fucktard warlocks let the honey badger go. My former cellmate Sassy the Assbag Witch from Hell is picking their brains as we speak. She has promised not to blow up my house, but it still remains to be seen. I am assuming the honey badger has come back to the area to get the solution and the syringe he used on Hildy when he killed her. As soon as we have the intel, I will make a plan. It will probably be a bad plan, but I will make it nonetheless. Any questions?"

"Um, are you going to leave us hanging?" Roger the rabbit asked.

"I've told you all I know at this point."

"I think he means hanging in the air," Mac supplied gently.

"Oh. I knew that," I said quickly.

"Like seven?" he inquired casually.

"Yes," I said in a business-like tone. "Exactly like seven. As to you guys hanging... I'm still figuring that one out, so..."

"What the hell is this?" Sassy grunted as she staggered across the yard looking like she'd ran the Boston Marathon and then gotten electrocuted. "Some kind of fucked up Shifter party ritual?"

The cats followed behind her, still singed from the earlier blast, but looking fine.

"Oh my Goddess." I gasped and grabbed Sassy before she face planted at my feet. "Are you okay?"

"Never been better. Is Jeeves here?"

Once a hooker, always a hooker.

"Nope, he's still at the grocery. He gets carried away there," Mac told her.

"That's slightly metrosexual," she said, confused.

"He's a chef," I added quickly before she started asking too many questions. She'd meet Jeeves soon enough. I just wanted to be there when she did.

"That's hot," she said.

The cats nodded their approval.

"Yes, well we have a few issues here," I said getting back on track. "I sort of accidentally suspended the Shifters. I would be very appreciative if you could undo the spell and let them down."

"My pleasure," she said.

With a wave of her hand all the Shifters dropped to the ground with resounding thuds and a whole bunch of moaning.

I'd hoped for a little more finesse, but we were dealing with Sassy.

"Mmmkay... well that's certainly one way to do it," I muttered.

"Hey," she barked. "None of them blew up."

"True, which leads me to the next question. Did you find the traitor?"

"Yes and no," she hedged.

"Spill it," I said with exasperation.

"Well, I think they all had something to do with it, but someone else was behind the plan. I think it's a witch."

"You *think*? What do you mean you *think*? You're supposed to *know*," I hissed.

"Dude, those fuckers are old," Sassy whined. "You cannot even believe the rancid shit I had to sift through to even get that much. However, they didn't want to do it. It seems like they had no choice."

"They were spelled?" I asked.

"Probably... since they can't remember," she said with a shrug.

"That doesn't make much sense," I said.

"No fucking kidding," she agreed.

"Actually it does make some sense," Simon said as he walked over.

"You are hot," Sassy cooed. "You seeing anyone?"

"Yes, he is seeing someone," I snapped. "Keep it in your pants. Simon what are you talking about?"

"I sense a witch in the area. It's not Hildy and it's not this one."

"Awesome," I yelled making everyone jump. "I have ten pissed off warlocks with memory loss in my basement, a honey badger on the loose, and a bad witch who can bend the warlock's wills flying around in my hood."

"Sucks for you," Sassy said.

"Nope," Mac corrected her. "It sucks for all of us. We're a team."

I wanted to jump him and make him see the Goddess. He was hotter than hell and he was mine. Wait. He was *not* mine. He was just someone I was dating temporarily. Riiiiiight.

Maybe I should talk to Roger.

No.

No.

No.

After I was done here I would go to Florida and do some intensive therapy—for a year. Yes. Good plan.

"Florida is too hot. It's filled with tourists and pelican Shifters. You would hate it there. Pelicans are violent bastards—lots of healing," Mac said with a raised brow and a hint of warning in his voice.

"Get out of my head," I said.

"Stop thinking so loud," he countered.

"Ohhhhhhhhh, he can read your mind?" Hildy squealed. "That means he's your…"

"STOP!" I yelled. "We have a problem here and it has to be handled."

Hildy just giggled. "Of course, dear. You're correct. Carry on."

I considered falling to the ground and banging my head, but I was unsure if I could heal myself without blowing up.

"What are we going to do, Boss Lady?" Sassy asked as she and my community stared at me and waited for my answer.

"We're gonna… um… kick some ass. I just need twenty-four hours to train and come up with a plan that doesn't result in the end of Assjacket and all its inhabitants. Until that time, I want everyone to bring tents here and camp out. I don't want anyone on their own until we're certain it's safe."

"I'm not going anywhere," Chuck, now back in his human form, said as he stood right beneath my Aunt. "I will protect what's mine and all of my friends."

Hildy sighed and blushed with joy.

"He's such an alpha," she murmured.

"Damn right, woman," Chuck said with the first real smile I'd seen in ages.

"Alrighty then, everyone go get your tents. I'm going inside to have a brief panic attack and then I'm going to watch Project Runway and eat a vat of cookie dough. Everything is going to be fine," I assured my people.

They all cheered and waved as they went home to get their camping gear.

I then prayed to the Goddess I wasn't selling them a bridge.

I prayed really hard.

Really, really hard.

Chapter 12

"Wait," I said as I wiped the sweat from my brow and tried to catch my breath. Magic training sucked. I wasn't sure what the five-mile run had to do with controlling my magic, but I did as I was told. "All the Shifters have gifts?"

"Oh yes," Hildy said as she flitted about in the air. "Wonderful gifts."

It was morning and we were in the back yard. All the Shifters were camped out in the front.

Behind the house was off limits while I practiced my magic with Daaaaad and Hildy. Sassy was supposed to join us, but her lazy ass slept in. I wasn't going to run the risk of hurting anyone.

Even Mac agreed to let me out of his sight for an hour or two.

"Wanda has the power to calm people," Daaaaad said. "Deedee promotes happiness."

"I can see those being true," I grunted as I tried to zero in on a small rock and obliterate it without creating a car-sized crater like I had only moments ago when I tried to make a leaf disappear.

"You'll want the lion Shifters to have a go at your yard in the near future," Daaaaad recommended as he examined one of the larger holes I'd blasted.

"Why?"

"Their gift is communing with the earth," Hildy said. "Very strenuous. It's why they sleep all the time."

"I always thought they were lazy," I said as I gave up on the rock and sighed. There were twelve large craters in my back yard. This was not going well.

"Oh, heavens no," Hildy said. "Just the opposite."

"Roger the rabbit is an empath," Daaaaad added without cracking a smile.

I wasn't as polite. My laugh burst from my lips and I bent over in hysterics. "Roger is not an empath. Roger's a porno addict."

A streak of vivid purple lightning, compliments of the Goddess, descended from the sky and zapped me right in the ass.

"Mother humper," I squealed as I rubbed the butt blast that I was certain would leave a scar.

"Sorry," I yelled to the heavens. "It slipped."

"Witch's Oath?" Hildy asked as she hovered low and examined my still smoldering rear end.

"Yep, I wasn't supposed to share that icky nugget."

"Oh sweetie, we all know about Roger's fondness for voyeurism. It doesn't preclude him from being a wonderful therapist. He's an outstanding sexual therapist."

"Yuck," I mumbled as I patted my singed backside. "Don't really want to hear it."

"I've considered speaking with him about tips on phone sex for Chuck and me," Hildy informed us.

"Gotta agree with Zelda on this one. Yuck. That's TMI, my sister," Daaaaad said as he winced."

"Whatever, Mr. I-Have-a-date-with-Baba-Yaga," Hildy sang gleefully. "I have waited for this for hundreds of years!"

"What are you talking about?" Daaaaad demanded.

"Fabio, you need to settle down with a nice witch. You have had the most appalling taste in women for centuries," she admonished.

"Product of horrid liaison here," I reminded my aunt with a raised hand.

"Oh dear," she muttered and turned agitated circles in the air. "You are a blessing. Your mother may have been horrid, but you my dear, are a gift."

"You knew her?" I asked.

"You could say that," she hedged.

"Spill," I insisted.

Hildy froze midair and wrinkled her brow. Goddess, she was exactly like her brother trying to find a creative way around the truth.

"I want facts, not fiction."

Hildy sighed dramatically and floated down to the earth. She kept her distance, but came as close as she felt was safe. My

ROBYN PETERMAN

stomach dropped. What other nasty things could I learn about the witch who spawned me?

"Well, about a hundred and seventy-two years ago, your mother and I had a little tiff."

"Little?" Daaaaad snorted. "You and she blew up a good portion of Southern California."

"And that would be because?" I asked wanting to know what would cause such violence.

"She was copying me," Hildy huffed as she flipped her brother off.

Grabbing a bottle of water, I pulled up a lawn chair and seated myself. "Let me get this straight. You destroyed part of a state because she was copying you?"

"It was more complicated than it sounds," Hildy explained. "It was like she was trying to be me. She dressed like me, mimicked my spells, borrowed my clothes, stole my journal…"

"And your boyfriend," Daaaaad added.

"Yes well, she was welcome to him. He was a spineless buttdonkey," she hissed.

"An ass-ass," I corrected her.

"What?" Hildy asked, perplexed as Daaaaad snickered.

"Nothing," I muttered. "So you blew up a state?"

"Not because of that. But when I caught her stealing hair out of my hairbrush it all came to a head," she ground out.

"Holy Goddess," I said with a shudder. "She took hair?"

Taking hair meant she was planning either a voodoo doll of Hildy, which was against every magical law on the books, or she was going to do a very evil spell on my aunt. Both were cowardly and abhorrent.

"She took my hair," Hildy hissed. "Of course I got it back."

"Didn't she also dye her own hair to match yours?" Daaaaad asked.

"She did. So I smited her ass and she smote right back. It got somewhat out of hand and we blew up a few things."

"Like a quarter of a state," Daaaaad mumbled.

"Whatever," Hildy snapped. "I won. She lost. She spent a good ten years in the pokey for what she tried to do."

"Like mother, like daughter," I said as I dropped my head into my hands.

"No. You killed me by accident," Fabio consoled me. "It didn't even hurt… much."

"I'm a loser," I moaned. "I can't handle my magic, and I ran over my dad and killed him."

"Luckily he was a cat, dear," Hildy said lovingly as if it was the one fact which mattered most. "Nine lives and all."

84

Wait a minute.

"So you boffed my mom knowing she had tried to kill your sister?"

I was shocked, completely grossed out and mad.

"Absolutely not," Daaaaaad said defensively. "I didn't even know her name when I first boffed her."

"Nice," Hildy said sarcastically.

"I didn't," Daaaaad insisted. "I was in Rome studying gymnastics when the showdown with your aunt happened. Your mother was going by an entirely different name a hundred years later when we met."

"Gymnastics?" I queried with a snicker.

"Talk to me when you've lived as long as I have," Daaaaad shot back. "Hobbies are hard to find."

Holy hell, what did I have to look forward to?

"He's right. I was into snake charming and fly-fishing before my demise. Anyhoo, I'm quite positive she knew you were my brother," Hildy told him. "We're kind of hard to miss with the red hair and all."

"Possibly," Daaaaad agreed. "She was quite obsessed with my healing abilities and wanted me to teach her."

"My mom is *not* a healer," I said in my outdoor voice. "I healed her daily for years. I thought it would make her like me better. It just pissed her off."

"I hear she's living with a Vampire," Hildy said with a derisive snort.

"This is true," I muttered somewhat distracted by everything I was learning.

Was my mother jealous of my abilities? I couldn't imagine why she would want to heal. She was as selfish as they came.

"Why on earth would my mother want to be a healer?" I asked. "She didn't have a lick of compassion in her."

"Isn't it obvious?" Hildy snipped. "With the healing power we're in line to become the next Baba Yaga."

"Wait. There's only one Baba Yucky and she's a 1980's reject." I was so confused.

"Oh dear." Hildy giggled. "Sometimes I forget how young you are and how little training you've had. Baba Yaga is simply a title bestowed on our chosen leader. Baba's real name is Carol."

"You're shitting me."

Carol? Her name was Carol? That just didn't compute.

"Do I look like I'm shitting you?" Hildy inquired seriously.

"Um… no. So healers are Baba Yagas?"

"Yes, there are two lines which can rule. Ours—the line with healers—or Carol's."

"What's Carol's line? The fashion disasters?" I asked with a giggle.

Hildy's belly laugh made me giggle harder. "No, no, no no!" She waved her finger at me as she tried to control her mirth. "Carol's line are creators."

"So we have special magic?" I asked.

"We do. Our magic can't be taught. It simply is," Hildy said with a flip of her red hair.

"Well, I sure as hell hope I can be *taught* to control this shit because the craters are ugly," I cut in referring to my destroyed back yard.

When Baba Yumpy showed up for her date with Daaaaad, I was going to have to stop myself from calling her Carol. In fact, it was going to be next to impossible.

"You just need to relax and focus," Hildy advised. "Stop thinking so hard. When you wanted the Shifters to stop beating themselves up, what did you do?"

"I waved my hand and wished for them to cease the idiocy," I said.

"There you go," Daaaaad said happily. "PS, Chuck has some real issues."

Hildy nodded and flew herself to the chair next to me. "He doesn't care about freezing to death. He wants to be with me."

"He's been trying to off himself for weeks," I told her.

"If he kills himself, he will never be with her," Daaaaad said thoughtfully. "His death must be natural or noble in order to move on to the Next Adventure."

I considered the question hovering on my tongue for a good while before I asked it. Did even I really want to know what was foremost in my mind? Could I handle the truth?

"Hildy?"

"Yes dear?"

"What is the Next Adventure like?"

"I haven't been there yet," she said quietly. "I was in a holding tank of sorts, I suppose. Apparently the Goddess had more plans for me here."

"So the Next Adventure could be nothing—just a big black hole of nothingness?" I whispered.

"Maybe," she answered. "But I don't think so. I caught little glimpses of those moving on and it was indescribable."

"Beautiful?" I inquired hopefully.

"Beyond mere words," she replied. "It looked and felt like pure peace."

"I don't want you to go there. I want you to stay," I said in a voice that reminded me of myself as a child begging my mom to love me.

Hildy floated close without touching and smiled at me. "My coming back is a gift," she said. "I don't know how long it will last, but meeting you completes me. I never had a child, but if I had one, I could only wish she was as beautiful, compassionate, kind and as strong as you."

"I'm none of those things," I told her.

"You are all of those things, child. You just have to believe."

Was she right? With all my bad traits—and there were many—was I all those good things too?

"This is getting deep," Daaaaad said as he hugged me tight.

"Yep," I said as I wiped away a stray tear which had fallen from my eye. "Let's get back to more gossipy shit. What's Chuck's gift?"

"You mean besides his prehensile lips?" Hildy inquired with a glint in her eye.

"What the hell does that mean?" I asked quite sure I would regret my question.

"Detachable lips! You wouldn't believe what he can do with those. One time..." Hildy was on a roll.

"Stop!" I yelled and smacked my hands over my ears. "I am this close to projectile hurling and I ate multi-colored cereal this morning for breakfast. And thank you for assuring for the need to tack on at least ten more years of therapy."

Daaaaad scrubbed his hands over his handsome face and groaned. "I think I might need some therapy to erase that one too."

"You're all just jealous," she trilled. "Don't you want to know Mac's gift?"

"No she does not," Daaaaad grumbled. "She going to meet a nice warlock and settle down. Soon."

"Hummph," Hildy grunted. "Warlocks are imbeciles. Present party included. A big, and I mean *big* Shifter, is definitely the way to go."

I bit back my laugh as Daaaaad turned an unbecoming shade of purple. Hildy sang on about the size of Shifters and I was certain Daaaaad was going to blow.

"What's Mac's gift?" I asked trying to avoid a brother-sister smackdown.

"Ohhhhhhh," Hildy said with reverence. "Mac has a gift very few are given. He was blessed by the Goddess with compassion and a deadly protective instinct unparalleled by any magical species. Shifters of his kind only come along every few thousand years. He is meant for greatness."

My stomach lurched and I wanted to cry.

Shitballsbuttbomb.

"Well, there you go," I choked out in a tone I hoped sounded casual and uncaring. "He needs to pick someone far better than me."

"He didn't pick you. You were meant for him," Hildy informed me.

"Oh my hell," I yelled. "So he's stuck with me? This is awful. He needs someone who can you know... be a responsible grown up."

"No, he just needs someone who will love him," Hildy countered simply.

This was giving me hives. Hildy did not understand. She didn't really know me. None of these people did.

Hell, I'd spent more time with Sassy in the pokey than any of my new friends—and Sassy didn't know me either. I wasn't sure *I* even knew me.

They thought I was nice and compassionate. I was not the witch they were making me out to be. This was far more than I could handle. Once they realized who I really was—a selfish, unstable, unlovable and materialistic nightmare they wouldn't want me anymore.

Fuck, this was why I never stayed anywhere long. It always ended in disappointment—usually mine. I was getting far too attached here and it was going to end in heartbreak. It most often did.

Fine. I was a big girl. I owed it to the community to find the evil and destroy it. Doing so would feel good and make me happy. After I was done, I would quietly slip away. Maybe Sassy could take over. No. That would be a clusterfuck. I would break up with Mac and let him know I wasn't mating material for him.

Goddess, if I did that I'd definitely have to leave. Seeing him with another woman would kill me... or I'd kill her. Not very kind and compassionate... or legal.

I narrowed my eyes and focused on the rock I'd given up on earlier. Before I could explore the ramifications of creating another massive hole in my yard, I blew up the rock. Only the rock. Bingo. Without much thought, I flicked my fingers and filled in all the craters. As an afterthought, I added a few trees and flowering shrubs.

Daaaaad was grinning and Hildy was cheering. I was about to conjur up an Olympic sized swimming pool, but stopped short. That was self-serving... wasn't it?

"Would a pool be a bad thing or a good thing?" I asked my next of kin.

"Will you open it to the community?" Daaaaad asked with a

smirk.

I considered for only a second. "Yes, but only in human form. I am not cleaning hair out of filters."

"Then I say yes!" Hildy squealed.

"Done." I wiggled my nose and a pool appeared. "I'm handling my magic," I shouted as I added twenty cabana chairs and a pool house complete with a snack shack and sauna.

This was fun. Goddess, I could fix up down town for the community and maybe even magic up a Target.

"Holy shit on a stick, you people are loud," Sassy shouted from her window above. All of your rude chattering woke me up an hour ago."

"Your point, lazy ass?" I yelled back.

"You need me," she said with a huge yawn.

"And yet again, I'm not following."

"The witch. The one behind stealing Hildy's magic is the very same one who sent the honey badgers to kill you. I know who it is."

"You gonna make me guess?" I snapped.

"Nope, but I have to pee like a race horse. Keep your panties on. I'll be down in five."

Chapter 13

"Is she sane?" Hildy asked as we waited for Sassy and her theory on who the witch was.

"Define sane," I muttered as I paced.

"Oh dear..." Hildy mumbled as she flew around and wrung her hands.

To pass the time while Sassy relieved herself, I added nice teak tables with sun umbrellas to the pool deck. I considered a diving board, but the amount of broken Shifter necks I'd have to heal prevented me.

"Where is she?" I hissed.

"Peeing," Daaaad reminded me.

"Duh. How long does it take to pee?" I snapped.

"Depends on the time of day and if it's hot or cold outside. Month of the year also is a determinate," he explained seriously.

"Alrighty then," I said and kept pacing.

Did she really have the answer we were looking for? How in the hell could she? Sassy wasn't from here and only knew the bare bones of what had gone on in the last several weeks. Had the warlocks told her and she'd held out? She was in for an enormous ass smite if that was the case.

"Dude, the guest bathroom has a water fountain in the toilet," Sassy said, stuffing a bagel in her mouth as she stumbled out into the backyard.

"Did you drink out of it?" I asked, suppressing an evil grin.

"No, am I supposed to?" she asked.

All the bathrooms in the house had bidets—very European. Clearly my Aunt Hildy had a thing for cleanliness.

"Yes. Yes you are. It's a very rare and tasty natural spring water," I said without cracking a smile.

"Seems a little odd to drink from a toilet, but whatever. When in Assjacket..." Sassy said with a shrug.

"Soooooo?" I asked.

"Wait. Do I just drink from it like a water fountain or do I get a glass and fill it?"

"Water fountain," I said as Daaaaad sprinted to the other side of the yard to hide his laughter.

"Is he okay?" Sassy inquired with concern. She wiped the cream cheese from her fingers onto some very expensive jeans which looked disturbingly like a pair of mine.

"He's fine," I said quickly. "Info please."

"It's not real hard to figure out, dumbass," she said. "You know her."

I knew her? Who in the hell did I know that Sassy knew as well?

"It's not Baba Yopaininmyass," I informed her firmly.

"Oh my Goddess." Sassy crouched over in laughter. "Of course it's not! She might be a fashion show disaster, but she's good through and through. A little rough on the punishments if you ask me, but she's not evil."

"Okay," I said as I ran my hands through my hair in frustration. "Who is it?"

"You don't want to guess?" she asked with a smirk.

"No," I ground out as I briefly considered magically rearranging her face. "I don't want to guess."

Sassy back away and grinned. "Don't do it," she warned.

"Do what?" I shouted.

"I don't know, but don't do it," she replied with a giggle.

She was enjoying herself way too much for my pleasure.

"I'll tell Jeeves you're into My Little Pony sexual role playing," I threatened.

"What the heyhey?" She gasped and backed further away. "How did you know that?"

"Holy shit," I choked out. "I made that crap up."

"Well, you have no room to talk, Little Red Riding Hood," Sassy accused.

"I most certainly do," I shot back. "A witch with a rainbow tail coming out of her ass and a witch wearing a ten thousand dollar Chanel red cape are two entirely different things."

"Mother *fucker*," Sassy gushed, totally impressed. "You have a ten thousand dollar cape?"

"I do," I squealed completely forgetting what we were talking about.

Daaaaad's groan and dry heave brought me back to reality.

"Okay," I reasoned trying to get back on track. "I will do my damnedest to block out that you like to wear a tail and snort during sex. And you will tell me who the fucking witch is. Now."

"You won't tell Jeeves?" she asked with narrowed eyes.

"No, I won't tell. Witch's Honor," I promised.

I heard Hildy's chuckle and I shot her a look that shut her up fast. My track record with Witch's Honor was slightly lacking lately.

"Good because I want to surprise him," Sassy said.

"He'll definitely be surprised," I said with a small shudder feeling sorry for Jeeves. He had no clue he was now in a relationship with Sassy the Horse. "The witch?"

"Oh right... it's your mom."

WTF?

"Did the butmunching warlocks tell you this?" I demanded as I advanced on her. My mother was a heartless skank, but not a killer. At least I didn't think so...

"No, your loud mouths did," she said as she stood her ground.

"Explain," I snapped.

Hildy had flown close and Daaaaad high tailed it back over.

"Let's start with something I'm curious about. What the hell is her name?" Sassy asked.

"Judith," I said at the same time Daaaaad said, "Sandy," and at the very moment Hildy said, "Isobelle."

"Okay." Sassy shook her head and chuckled. "I'm just gonna stick with 'your mom'."

"Out with it," I said impatiently.

"She's dating a Vamp?" she asked.

"Yes, what does that have to do with anything?" Daaaaad asked, perplexed.

"I'll get to that," Sassy promised. "You're hot. Are you seeing anyone?" she asked him with a lecherous smile

"Oh my hell," I hissed. "He's my daaaaad."

"Ooops, sorry. That *is* a little weird," she agreed. "And anyway, I'm dating Jeeves."

I held my tongue before I reminded her she hadn't even met Jeeves yet, but there was no time for a debate. I needed answers.

"So, your mom tried to be Hildy, right?" Sassy asked.

"Right," Hildy answered.

"Then dated your daaaaad and tried to learn to heal?"

"Yes, but boffed would be more accurate," Daaaaad chimed in.

"Okay, boffed," Sassy amended. "Got pregnant with his child?"

"Yes," I said as my head felt light. She was on to something. I could feel it in my gut. I just couldn't decipher the details.

"Hated you?" she asked me.

"Yes," I admitted softly.

"Wanted to be a Baba Yaga?" she added. "Which by the way, I didn't know about either."

"The Baba thing being a title?" I asked, glad I wasn't the only one.

"Who did your training dear?" Hildy asked kindly.

"I was home schooled," Sassy told her.

"By a witch?" Hildy asked.

"Nope, by me," Sassy said with pride.

Well that certainly explained a lot.

"Sassy, while all of this is somewhat revolting to discuss, I'm not sure I see how you came to this conclusion," Hildy said as she made the international kookoo sign behind Sassy's back.

"I can see how you would say that," Sassy agreed with a nod.

"Wait, the revolting part or the how in the hell did you cook up this bizarre plot part?" I asked getting confused and more annoyed.

"Both," Sassy confirmed.

"Sassy," Daaaaad ground out as calmly as he could. "It would be outstanding if you could put us out of our misery here. Get to the damn point."

"Right," she said. "She couldn't get it by imitation. She couldn't get it by boffing. She couldn't get it by bearing a child from the healer line."

"Get what?" I asked.

"Your magic," she said with an eye roll.

"Your point?"

"She can't be a healer without your magic. Therefore she can't be a Baba Yaga. I'm pretty sure it's what she's always been after. By the way, it's still blowing my mind that Baba's name is Carol. She is so not a Carol. It should be Madonna or Cyndi Lauper or Pat Benatar."

"So true," I agreed and then slapped myself in the head for losing concentration again. Sassy could make the Devil himself lose focus.

"Anyhoo, the badgers got your magic," she told Hildy.

"Would you like to tell us something we don't know," Hildy queried less politely than usual.

"Wait. You think my mother was behind the badgers?" I

gasped.

"Possibly or maybe not. But it certainly seems like she knew enough to let the ugly rubbery fucker go."

"I thought the creepy little warlocks did that," Daaaaad said.

"For fucks sake, do I have to spell out everything?" Sassy huffed.

"Yes," we yelled in unison causing Sassy to jump, resulting in half of the cabana blowing up.

"Whoops." Sassy giggled and shrugged. "Your mother dates a vamp, right?"

"Pretty sure we've already clarified that icky nugget," I reminded her.

"That explains it," she said with a satisfied grunt like she was done.

"Oh. My. Hell," I shouted and flung my arms, inadvertently blowing up the other half of the cabana. "Explains what?"

"The puncture wounds in the necks of the douchehole warlocks," she replied as if we were daft.

My knees buckled and I dropped to the ground with a thud. Sassy was brilliant—a massive pain in my ass—but brilliant. The answer was right in front of us.

"It doesn't prove she was behind the whole thing," I said as I expelled the breath I'd been holding.

"No," Sassy agreed. "But I'd bet my finest tail, the one with all the sequins and feathers sewn on it, that she's involved now."

Again I almost forgot what I was talking about as the visual of Sassy's horsetail invaded my brain. Her mind alone was a weapon which could be used to kill.

"I'm still not on the same page," Daaaaad said.

"The vampire bit all the warlocks and tranced them into making them let the badger go. He probably wiped their memory of it too. That's why they can't remember," I told him.

"Do you think he bit the badger too?" Sassy asked.

"Um… that would be insanely gross, but I don't know," I said. "A couple of theories could work here. One—the badgers worked with my mother to get Hildy's magic. However, that didn't pan out because the badger put the magic in himself. Two—my lovely maternal incubator heard about it and wants the ability to do it herself. She'd have to have the honey badger to get the syringe."

"Diabolical, but certainly possible," Daaaaad said.

"Goddess, I should have smited her to dust all those years ago," Hildy hissed.

"No," Sassy disagreed. "If you had, I wouldn't have a best

friend. Zelda would have never been born."

Hildy turned a ghostly ashen and dropped down to the ground next to me. "She's right," she apologized. "I didn't mean what I said."

"I know," I told my aunt. "And you." I pointed at Sassy. "Are you just trying to butter me up or are you trying to make me go easy on the fact you smeared fucking cream cheese on my jeans?"

"Both?"

"Smart girl," Daaaaad said as his hands lit up with sparks. "Let's go find your mother. I have a few things I'd like to tell her in sign language."

"Nope," I said firmly as I stood up and gave Sassy a quick, awkward hug. "We go after the badger. It'll be easier to find a stinky animal than a witch who doesn't want to be found until she has the syringe. Plus she's most likely working with a vampire."

"It's next to impossible to kill a vamp," Hildy worried aloud.

"It might be difficult to find the honey badger too," I said.

"Can we scry for him?" Sassy asked.

"Excellent suggestion," Daaaaad said. "However, scrying can take days and I don't think we have days."

"We don't need to scry," Hildy announced. "There's a Shifter with the gift of being able to sniff out other species, but..."

"But what?" I asked, excited to have a lead.

"It's Bo," Hildy said softly.

"Baby Bo?" I shouted in disbelief. "Four year old, adorable Bo?"

"Yes," she answered. "He is an alpha in training. His power is immense."

"Absofuckinglutely not. He's too young and I won't risk his life. The honey badgers have already cracked his skull. And let me just say, it hurt like a motherhumper from hell to heal that wound," I snapped. "There has to be another way. Sassy go find a mirror and start to scry. Daaaaad go with her since she's never seen the honey fucker. Hildy start thinking of a plan B which doesn't involve a child."

"Zelda, this might be the only way. It might be what fate decrees," Hildy said sadly.

"Then fate can bite my butt. There's always another way. I just have to figure out what the hell it is," I insisted. "And I *will* figure it out."

Shitshitshit. I just hoped I wasn't blowing smoke up my own ass.

Chapter 14

"I can do it," Little Bo said sweetly as he puffed out his tiny chest and growled.

I ran my hands through my hair and paced the front lawn in agitation. All the Shifters gave me a wide berth as my fingers were shooting off green sparks.

"I think we can find a better and safer way," I said. "You're simply too young to deal with a witch, a vampire and a honey badger."

Mac leaned against the railing of my front porch and watched the action with his arms crossed over his chest. I didn't recognize the expression on his face, but didn't have time to decipher it. The Shifters were whispering and I was getting annoyed.

"I'm not crazy about this," Wanda said as she held her son close. "But my boy is correct. Bo is capable."

"He's just a baby," I yelled. "The honey badgers almost killed him the last time."

"But they didn't," Mac said from the porch. "Shifters are vastly different than humans and much different than witches. Plus we have the Shifter Whisperer."

"That's Shifter Wanker," I ground out.

"My bad," he said biting his lip to suppress his grin.

I was tempted to blow up part of the porch—the part that would land on his head. He was supposed to be on my side, especially if he wanted in my pants. What was happening here?

"He's four," I snapped.

"He's an alpha," Mac countered.

The plethora of Shifters in my yard went silent and watched the unfolding drama between the witch and the wolf.

"You would risk a child's life? A child from your kingdom?"

"I wouldn't risk any of my people's lives," Mac said coolly. "Ever."

"Not having puppies with you," I muttered under my breath.

The next thing I knew the wolf was in my personal space, I was trapped against his hard body and his lips were at my ear.

"Do not judge things you don't understand, Zelda. You are young and inexperienced. Trust me on this. I don't want our people to see us at odds. It will not be helpful," he whispered.

A chill of desire and a shudder of fury skittered through my body. I was torn and I didn't like Mac one little bit at the moment. My attraction to him infuriated me. I was a dummy. I knew he was right about hiding the dissenting opinions, but I couldn't cave where Bo was concerned—alpha Shifter or not.

"No, I won't allow it," I informed him loud enough to be heard.

The gasps from the crowd made me uneasy and the power radiating off the man I was challenging didn't bode well. Mac was a force that any sane person wouldn't reckon with. I was clearly insane.

"I can't heal a dead person," I argued to the Shifters and ignored the sexy assbucket who had attached himself to me. "He's just a little boy."

Wanda and Simon carefully approached with Hildy floating above. I pushed Mac away—actually I was fairly sure he let me. It was as if everyone was against me and I hated that feeling.

A big part of me wanted to throw my hands in the air and say "fuck all of you" then leave. I really wanted to do that. But I was supposed to watch over these imbeciles. They were making it very hard.

"Zelda," Hildy explained. "Mac is right. Shifters are not like us. They're people, but they're also animals. Their instincts and gifts are very different from ours. Bo will not be alone, but he's the only one who can scent the honey badger. The longer we wait, the more danger we're in."

Wanda took my hands in hers. "He's my son. It humbles me you feel so strongly about him, but what has been said is true. Bo is powerful and will be protected."

"I know this seems odd to you," Simon said kindly. "But this is the way it is for us."

"Who will protect him?" I demanded.

"I will," Chuck said as he stepped forward from the crowd. "Not a hair on his head will be harmed."

"You'll protect him?" I asked doubtfully.

"With my life," Chuck promised.

"Well that certainly doesn't help." I laughed and the crowd backed further away. The sparks now covered the entire top half of my body. "You've been trying to end your life for weeks."

Chuck bowed his head and stayed silent.

"Look, I'm sorry, but you have," I told him.

"This is true, but my duty to my people comes before my desire to be with my mate."

"He's your mate?" I asked Hildy, totally surprised as I tamped my magic down.

She nodded and hovered above Chuck.

"He bit you?" I asked.

Hildy nodded again and winked.

"Did it hurt?" I asked much to the amusement of the town witnessing me and my filter-less mouth.

"Just the opposite," she said with an enormous grin.

I felt Mac at my back and moved away. It didn't matter if was orgasmically awesome. It didn't matter if it tickled. It wasn't going to happen for me. Not with Mac. Not with anyone. I was leaving. I would fight with everything I had and then disappear.

Too many feelings were fucking with my chi.

I'd miss Assjacket and its inhabitants, but I'd get over it. I always did.

And the truth was they'd be better off without me. So if this was the way they wanted to do it, who was I to stop them? They'd do it with me or without me.

"We can't do it without you," Mac said as he again moved into my personal space. "It's not possible."

Again I moved away. "Fine... and get out of my head," I said. The Shifters heaved a collective sigh of relief. "We'll do it your way, but as soon as we find the badger, I want Bo moved to safety."

"That's a given," Mac said.

I refused to make eye contact with him. His eyes spoke more than his mouth and I was concerned he heard all of what I'd just thought. Tough shit. If he was rude enough to crawl into my head, he'd just have to deal with what he heard.

"Alright," I said. "I want all the strongest fighters to gather in groups of five. Once we know the location, we'll have the groups surround the area and we'll go in together."

"Hey, I suck at scrying," Sassy yelled as she pushed her way through the crowd.

Daaaaad followed behind her looking like he wanted to pull his hair out. Sassy was good like that.

"No worries," I said. "We have a change of plans. You and Daaaaad will be coming with me. We might need to combine magic if we have to deal with a vamp. Where are the cats?"

"Eating," she snorted.

"Of course they are," I said with a disgusted shake of my head. If they were going to live here, they were going on a diet.

"Combining your power won't work," Hildy fretted. "Magic won't kill a vampire. Magic doesn't work on the already dead."

"What kills them?" I asked, afraid of the answer.

"Removing their head or staking their heart with silver," Daaaaad supplied gravely.

"I can remove a head with magic," I said as the bile rose in my throat.

I was a fucking healer—not a killer. This was against everything that I believed in. However, I could and would do it if my people were in danger.

"It must be done with bare hands or teeth," Wanda explained with a grimace.

"Alrighty then," I choked out. "I'm not your man."

"I'm your man," Mac said tersely.

The double entendre was not lost on me, but I ignored it. He could not be my man. He was too good for somebody like me.

"The blood will kill you," Daaaaad warned. "Even a drop will destroy you."

"I thought you didn't like him," I interrupted.

"I never said I didn't *like* him," Daaaaad replied in his defense. "I just don't like him with you."

"Got ya," I said with a nod.

Mac growled and my Daaaaad grinned.

"The blood won't kill Mac," Little Bo said reverently as he took his mom's hand and giggled. "Mac has more magic than anyone I know—super powers."

All the Shifters dropped to their knees and bowed their heads in respect. I turned and stared at the man who I secretly adored.

"Who are you?" I asked.

"Besides yours, I suppose you could call me a freak of nature," he said evenly.

"Hey," Sassy said in her outdoor voice even though she was a foot away. "Is my man Jeeves here?"

The Shifters glanced around nervously. Apparently they'd heard about Sassy's new fictional relationship and were terrified for poor Jeeves.

"Yes, I'm here," Jeeves shouted from the back of the crowd. "Does someone require servicing?"

"Oh shit," I muttered as Sassy squealed with glee.

"I do," she sang out as Jeeves emerged from the group. "Oh my Goddess, you're hot!"

I was unsure if she was seeing the same thing I was. Jeeves was far from hot. He was a hot mess. However, Jeeves was struck dumb as he bounced and stared at Sassy with undisguised lust.

"What the hell?" Mac muttered as Sassy grabbed Jeeves by the collar of his ill-fitted tux and laid a big wet one on him.

The Shifters clapped politely and looked confused.

"Looks like you've gained a daughter-in-law." I laughed at the look of horror on Mac's face.

"Looks like you have too," he shot back with a smirk.

I shrugged. I wasn't staying. Although the new turn of events was enough to make me leave alone. There wasn't enough money in the world to make me become related to Sassy—even by marriage.

Mac watched me with narrowed eyes and thin lips. When I stayed mute, he took over.

"The badger won't be out until after sundown. That gives us about eight hours to prepare," Mac directed. "Go to your tents and rest. I want everyone to eat and sleep. This is going to be a long night."

"Why not go after him while he's sleeping?" Simon raised his hand and asked.

"Because we need him to lead us to the syringe and ultimately to my mother," I said.

"Your mother?" Wanda asked with concern.

"I'll get them up to speed while Jeeves gives me a back rub that will lead to some afternoon delight," Sassy stated very seriously. "You go rest, boss lady."

"Mmmkay," I said warily. I wondered what Sassy's version would include and decided to block out the afternoon delight part.

"Oh and you were right. The spring water fountain rocks!"

I swallowed the burst of laughter that threatened to escape my lips and headed quickly for the house.

"What are you going to do, your Majesty?" a Shifter shouted out.

"I'm going to have a nap with my mate," he replied.

That stopped me dead. "I am *not* your mate," I hissed and slapped my now fire shooting hands on my hips. "And I am not sleeping with you."

"Who said anything about sleeping?" Mac inquired with a lopsided grin as all the Shifters hooted and hollered.

"I can smite all of you," I threatened, but they just laughed and kept cheering.

I'd take Mac to my room and let him have it. If he thought it was going to be pleasurable, he had another thing coming. He was dealing with a pissed off witch.

If he was smart, he'd run.

Mac scooped me up in his arms and marched toward the house.

Apparently, he was not smart.

Chapter 15

"You're smoking crack if you think you're going to get any, douchenozzle," I informed the idiot as he dumped me on my bed and began removing his clothes.

Silently and with a half smile, Mac continued until he was in his birthday suit. I stared at the ceiling. He was not fighting fair. His naked body sent my entire lower half into a tizzy.

"Cover your Bon Jovi or I'll zap him off," I threatened as I scrunched my eyes shut and put my hands over them for good measure. The visuals were far too tempting.

One side of the bed depressed and I rolled to the middle as Mac and his huge bare-naked frame made himself comfortable next to me. His scent alone was dangerous, but I knew if I opened my eyes I was done for.

"We're not having sex," I snapped as I tried to roll away.

He was quick and pinned me beneath him.

"Why?" he asked as he buried his face in my neck and nipped.

"Because I don't like you," I replied breathlessly as my girly parts began to take over my brain.

"But I like you," he said as he pressed his rock hard Jon Bon Jovi into my hip. "I like you a whole bunch."

"Liking me and wanting in my pants are two entirely different things," I said as I attempted to wiggle free.

"Not for me," he said.

I stayed silent and digested that one.

"Zelda, tell me why you're mad."

"Because," I said.

"Not an answer," he murmured as his fingers deftly unbuttoned my shirt. "And if you really want me to, I'll stop."

I didn't want him to stop. I wanted to open my eyes and take in his beauty. I wanted his arms around me and his strong body inside mine. I wanted him as much as I wanted my next breath. But I was mad.

"You undermined me. You went over my head in front of everyone. I thought we were working as a team."

"We are." Mac sat up and pulled my hands from my eyes. "If I started chanting spells and trying my hand at magic, what would you do?" he asked.

"Um... laugh?" I offered as I sat up too.

"Why?"

"Because you wouldn't know what you were doing. You could hurt yourself or someone else. Magic is some serious shit," I told him. I was hoping he wasn't going to give it a try just to prove a point I already got, but wasn't willing to concede.

"I didn't laugh at you," he stated.

"No, you didn't," I agreed and sighed heavily. "It's just that Bo's a child. No one ever stood up for me as a child. I wanted to protect him."

"Him or you?" Mac asked, running his large hand through my hair and smoothing it off my face.

Good question.

"I would be doing more harm to Bo and my people by protecting them from what they're to become," Mac said. "Bo will be protected. Will he be in any danger? Yes. Yes, he will. But we live our lives hidden from humanity. We live in a constant state of danger. To deny it or pretend it doesn't exist would be deadly. I never intended to let him fight or do anything else other than lead us to the hideout. Period."

I hated when he made sense. I hated it more that my own childhood had clouded my judgment. Was I going to have to cave and book a visit with Roger the boob-ogling therapist before I left? Goddess, what was happening to me?

"I'm sorry," I mumbled as I shut my eyes again and flopped back down on the bed. Even if I did accept I *was* his mate, I was going to screw it up. It couldn't be good form to backtalk the King in front of the kingdom.

"Zelda, you're strong, you're good and you're opinionated. You're a beautifully complicated challenge. It's not a bad thing for your compassion to outweigh your judgment occasionally. It's only dangerous if you follow through without really understanding the consequences."

"How'd you get so smart?"

"Well, I'm a little older than you," he replied as he gathered me in his strong arms and pressed his lips to my temple.

"Yeah... like older than dirt," I said with a smile pulling at my lips.

"Possibly," he agreed with a sexy smirk. "But I've stayed in very good shape."

He flexed his considerable arm muscles and I was torn between rolling my eyes and drooling.

"Touch me. I need you," he said softly.

I wanted to so very badly, but it would only make it more difficult to leave.

"You need someone who can be a queen and not embarrass you. You need someone smarter and more mature and more... just more."

"No. I need you," he said in a husky voice that humbled me and made me want to cry. "I've fallen in lo..."

"*No*," I blurted out and put my hand over his mouth. "Don't go there. You don't really know me."

I needed to run. I needed to crawl out of my skin. He was offering me what I desperately wanted, but couldn't have. He was making a mistake and I had to stop him. I was not lovable.

"I might know you better than you know yourself," he said as he pulled me even closer.

Brain or lady bits? Which one did I listen to? They were both quite loud at the moment, but the wahooha was slightly louder. Maybe this could be my last memory of us. I could take it with me and cherish it forever.

Was that fair? No. It wasn't fair to him or me, but it felt so right.

"Mac," I said as my brain and heart nobly tried to quash the need of my desire. "I don't think I can be your mate."

I held my breath and waited for him to get up and leave. It would tear my heart to bits, but it was the mature and responsible thing to do. God, being unselfish sucked ass.

"I'm aware you believe that," he said as he gently twisted a strand of my red hair in his fingers and played with it. "But you promised me fifteen death free dates. I want them all before you're allowed make a final decision. We're only on number eight. Are you reneging on your word?"

"Um..."

Shit. He had me there.

"No," I said and slapped my forehead.

"So just in case we all bite it tonight, I need to make love to you," he said as he made quick work of removing my shirt and pants.

I shivered and it wasn't because I was only clad in a sexy pair of panties and a barely there bra. His expression caused my shudder. His lids were hooded and his lust unmistakable. His breathing was heavier and his body tense.

"You're so beautiful," I murmured as I ran my fingertips through the light sprinkling of dark hair on his chest.

"I don't hold a candle to you," he replied as his lips found my collarbone and began to slide lower.

My back arched wantonly as he pulled the cup of my bra down and latched onto my nipple. The firm pulls from his lips went straight to my toes and the moan that left my mouth begged for more.

He smelled like heaven, all soapy, sexy man. He pulled back and stared as if he was trying to memorize me and I did the same. My heart was heavy in my throat as he traced my bottom lip with his finger and watched his motion with intensity.

"Mac…"

"Nope, no more talking unless it's you begging me to fuck you or praising me to the Goddess."

He grinned and without any problem unhooked my bra and flung it to the floor.

"I don't think I want to fuck you," he said.

My eyes shot to his in disappointment and shock as he chuckled and shredded my panties with no effort.

"Let me clarify," he said as he lowered himself over me. "We are definitely going to fuck, but not until I've made love to every inch of your gorgeous body. We clear?"

I couldn't speak, let alone think. And I was fairly sure I'd stopped breathing. "Gonna faint," I gasped out.

"You'll faint," he agreed with a smug sexy grin. "However, it won't be until you've come so many times you'll have no choice."

"You're certainly confident," I shot back in a shaky voice. My heart pounded so loudly in my chest, I was sure he could hear it.

"I don't make promises I can't keep, pretty girl. Never have, never will."

Holy shit, he wasn't joking.

He lowered his head between my legs and held me motionless as I gasped and tried to move. My hips wanted to thrust, but his hands held me like a vice. The sensation was so intense I wanted to scream.

"Goddess, Mac," I hissed as my body verged on orgasm.

"I'd prefer to be called a God, but I'll take what I can get."

He upped the ante and used his fingers and tongue in ways I didn't know were possible. The screaming was mine and only made him intensify and speed his process. Glittering golden magic gently rained down around us as I was unable to hold back. I trembled and moaned under his expertise. He'd definitely ruined for other men.

"Please," I begged as a heat coiled between my legs and the pressure threatened to undo me.

"Very polite," he said gruffly as he pinched my swollen clit between his fingers causing me to see stars. "But I have no clue what you want."

Goddess, he was a dick—a sexy, well hung wanker.

"Please, you know what I want," I insisted as I pressed my legs together to trap his hand and keep it where I wanted it.

"Beg," he demanded as he lowered his head to my breast and nipped.

"I don't beg," I shot back as my hips undulated and belied my words.

"Today you do."

His mouth replaced his fingers and he bit down and then sucked. The orgasm tore through me like a storm and my body thrashed and twisted. He went right back to work on me as the tingling ebbed and ramped me back to the place I couldn't control.

"Beg," he hissed as he ran his tongue from my belly button to my heavy aching breasts.

"Fuck me," I whispered.

"Can't hear you," he ground out and positioned his cock against my wet and needy opening.

"Please fuck me," I screamed as he pushed the head of his cock into me.

"So fucking tight," he ground out and then stilled.

The feeling of fullness was like a drug I couldn't live without. I dug my nails into his broad shoulders and tried to push my body onto his, but he held me fast.

"Again," he directed as he eased a little more of himself into me.

"Please, please, please fuck me," I cried out and bit at his lips which hovered above mine.

He was such a bastard. He pushed another inch into me, but it wasn't enough. I wanted all of him.

"Tell me you're falling in love with me," he snarled as he rotated his hips and sent me into a brain cell losing mini orgasm.

"You suck," I hissed and raised my hips to force him to give me more.

"Say it, Zelda. Or are you a coward?"

He continued to rotate his hips and sucked at my neck so

hard I knew it would leave a mark. I wanted him to slam his body into mine. I needed him to stop talking about love and just fuck me. Love was beyond me. I didn't understand it. I'd never had it. He was cheating so badly, but I couldn't think.

"I'm not a coward, you assmonkey," I snapped as I arched and rubbed my breasts against his chest.

His quick harsh intake of breath was way sexy beyond words. I grinned and tightened my body around his partially embedded cock and I squeezed hard. His eyes rolling back in his head was exactly what I wanted to see and I contracted even harder.

"Son of a bitch," he moaned and buried himself to the hilt with a swift and violent thrust.

He was almost too big to handle, but my body softened and gave its approval. My eyes closed and vivid colors ripped across my vision as he began to move. My hips joyously met each staccato thrust as he powered his way into my body, heart and soul.

"You're mine," he informed me in a tone usually obeyed by his subjects. But I was not one of his subjects…

"For now," I countered and wrapped my legs around his waist.

He laughed and kissed me soundly. "For always," he whispered.

The speed of his thrusts increased and he began to fuck me like the animal he was. It was so perfect, I thought I would lose my mind. I gasped in astonishment as he withdrew, but before I could utter a word he flipped me over to my hands and knees and slammed back into me.

"Got to be closer," he growled as he leaned forward and ran his fangs along the back of my neck.

He felt bigger. It was too much and too wonderful at the same time. I was his—in this moment and probably always. I knew I had to leave, but he would always own my heart.

"You're perfect," he murmured as he ran his fingers down my back.

"Far from it," I said as fell forward onto my outstretched arms, giving him even better access to my body.

"Perfect for me," he hissed as his speed ramped up to something that should have torn me apart.

I gloried in his possession and pumped back against his thrusts sending us both into an unstoppable frenzy. My power of speech and rational thought left me as an explosive orgasm ripped through me. Mac howled as he joined me.

I felt like Alice falling down the rabbit hole as wave after wave of tingling pleasure consumed my body. For a brief moment everything turned black.

"I think I fainted," I said with surprise.

"Told ya so," Mac replied with total male satisfaction.

I rolled my eyes and giggled. He certainly didn't break his promises. Mac rolled us to our sides. Still buried deep inside me, he spooned me and kissed my hair and neck over and over.

I felt a warmth inside me that I'd didn't understand. It was simultaneously tempting and terrifying. I tensed and tried to get up.

"No you don't," Mac said as he held tight. "I get to cuddle now."

"Alpha werewolves don't cuddle," I said.

"This one does," he countered with a laugh and playfully bit my neck. "Soon," he whispered.

I knew what he meant and ignored it. He was telling me that soon I would let him bite me for real. I wasn't going to set him straight. That would entail me telling him I was leaving which would cause a fight we didn't have time to deal with. I just wanted to be happy for a few more days. Arguing with Mac didn't fit into my plans.

"I'm kind of worn out," I said with a giggle. "Do we have time for a nap?"

"We do, beautiful girl," he replied as he grabbed a blanket and pulled it over us. "Go to sleep. I've got you."

I knew he did and he knew he did. He just didn't realize it was only for a day or so more.

I stopped thinking and closed my eyes just in case he was eavesdropping in my head. Sometimes the truth wasn't the best way. The truth could hurt. Often it was simply better to avoid the truth.

Trust me on that one.

I was an expert.

Chapter 16

"We don't have to go anywhere," Bo said with childlike certainty as he sniffed the air.

What the hell was he talking about? I knew this was a horrid idea. He was scared and didn't want to do it. He was only four—alpha or not.

Night had fallen and the Shifters were in groups of five ready to fight. The magic weighed heavy on the breeze and I had a bad feeling in my gut. Why did they all have to be involved? Someone was bound to get hurt or even die. If my mother was behind this, I should be doing this solo.

"Wait," I yelled into the tense silence. "This is my problem. I'm the one who's supposed to find the syringe and solution. I can handle this alone."

"I call bullshit," Fat Bastard grunted as he, Boba Fett and Jango Fett waddled up to my feet. "We are now your familiars and we want a piece of the action, Sweet Cheeks."

"I want to put a kink in someone's ass," Jango informed me seriously.

"I'm itchin' to do some bitchin'," Boba Fett added as not to be left out.

"That doesn't make any sense," I told him.

"It rhymed, didn't it?" he huffed as if I'd mortally wounded him.

"Well... yes."

"Alrighty then," he grumbled, now satisfied. "You fight. We fight."

"Okay," I said, very relieved. They were certifiable furry

shields from hell and I needed them. "Can anything hurt you?"

"Just you if you don't keep us," Jango said.

"They're really wonderful," Hildy chimed in as she floated above the cats who blew her wet kisses. "They just eat a lot. Oh, and don't let them start a poker club."

"Awwww, come on," Fat Bastard whined. "I already won half a million off the ugly magic gnome fuckers in the basement."

"Interesting," Daaaaad said as he rubbed his hands together with a look of child-like excitement in his eyes.

I now knew how Naked Dude made his fortune. We'd have to discuss it at a later date.

"Holy shit, I forgot about the warlocks," I said and began to pace. "Do you think the warlocks can be trusted? Can we use them?"

"Debatable," Sassy stated. "However, if you threaten their nads, I think you could control them."

"Worked on me," Jeeves announced happily.

"Isn't he adorable?" she squealed.

I had nothing.

"This is not just your problem," Mac said firmly as he stepped forward.

All of the Shifters nodded and stood taller.

"We're a team," Simon said. "You are not a lone wolf anymore. Well, you're not actually a wolf at all, but what I meant…"

"We know what you meant, Simon," Mac said kindly as Simon blushed and moved back to his group. "You're not alone anymore, Zelda. Not today and not ever again."

Goddess, I wanted to believe him, but getting people killed was not something I could stomach. I liked—or kind of maybe possibly loved these dumbasses—enough to choose to die in their place. Why couldn't anyone understand?

"I really think…" I started.

"They're coming here! Soon," Little Bo yelled and ran to his mom.

"What?" I shouted, stunned. Why were they coming here?

"Spread out and hide in the tree line in a circular pattern around the house," Mac commanded as I still tried to figure out why they were headed this way.

"Wanda," Mac continued. "Take Bo, the rest of the children and the oldest Shifters to the basement. You'll be safe there."

"What about the Warlocks?" Daaaaad asked as he put his hand up to halt Wanda and the rest.

He had a fine point, but a solvable point.

"Sassy, you go to the basement with them. The warlocks are

terrified of you. Daaaaad, you go too. I want the weaker protected," I instructed, back in business mode. "Sassy, threaten their testicles or tell them you'll ransack their brains again. I don't care."

No time to discern motive. I had to live in the moment. Hopefully I would live period.

"But I wanted to smite some fuckers," Sassy complained and stamped her foot causing part of the front porch to crumble.

"And I want you to do as I say," I snapped.

"Dang it," she groused. "Next time I get to smite the bad guys. And I get to keep your jeans."

"Fine," I told her.

"If there is a next time," I added under my breath.

"There will be," Mac assured me. "Chuck, team A and the cats get behind bushes around the house and conceal yourselves. No one touches the vampire but me. Zelda, can you do a spell that will cloak the scent of our people?"

"On it," I said having no clue if I could.

I took a deep breath and let her rip.

"Goddess on high, hear my call
Save the good from evil and don't let them fall
Cover, um... the damn scent with this improvised spell
Cloak them in magic, get rid of the smell"

I waved my hands in a confident circular motion and prayed it worked. Mac sniffed the air and grinned.

"Perfect, baby," he said with a quick slap to my ass.

Daaaaad's grunt of disapproval at Mac's display made me giggle, but the reality of what was to come sobered me. After an 'I'm the dad and I'm gonna kick your ass' glance at Mac, Daaaaad led Sassy and the others to the house.

"I think you should have said 'fucking spell'," Fat Bastard advised without cracking a smile. "Those dudes stink."

"Pot, kettle, black," I told him, still enjoying the fact it worked.

"Use my magic—it's inside you," Hildy urged as she flew above me.

"I though I had been," I told her. What was she talking about? I had more shit inside me I didn't know about?

"No," she said. "You haven't pulled deep enough to find it."

"Oh my hell," I snapped. "How will I know the difference?"

"My magic feels orange," she replied as she wrung her hands.

I was struck dumb. What in the Goddess's name did *orange*

feel like? Also, I didn't take the wringing of the hands as a good sign.

Motherhumpercowballs.

"You'll recognize it," she promised. "It's yours. It belongs to you. I believe in you, my child."

If only...

If Hildy had been my mother my life would have been vastly different. Wait. That was actually a disgusting thought. It would mean she'd done the nasty with her brother. Oh my hell, I needed to stop thinking altogether. My wandering mind was dangerous to my gag reflex.

In the distance I heard a car. They were driving up? That was ballsy.

"Either arrogance or stupidity," Mac said hearing the same thing I did.

"Why are they coming here?" Chuck asked as he popped out from behind a large bush.

"That's the question of the hour," I said as I tried to feel around for something orange in my gut.

Nothing.

Shit.

"Are we going to stand out in the open?" I asked Mac.

"Yep."

"Any reason?"

"Nope," he replied. "Just thought it would be polite to greet our guests."

I rolled my eyes and flicked my fingers rendering Mac and me invisible to all but each other—and apparently Hildy as she squealed with glee.

"It will only last ten minutes at the most," she reminded me.

"I know, but it might give us the edge to see what they're up to," I said as I made sure all the rest were hidden.

"Will they be able to see you?" I asked her.

"Only if I want them to," she replied with an evil little giggle.

"Can you freeze them?" I asked.

"But of course," Hildy said with a smirk.

Well, as far as preparation went, I thought we had it covered. One bad witch, one undead boyfriend and a honey badger. How hard could this be?

Never ever count your chickens before they hatch.

A convoy of military trucks approached my long drive way. There had to be at least seven and they were loaded with honey badgers.

"Looks like they rounded up reinforcements," Mac growled

as we watched the incoming vehicles.

"Fuck," I muttered and tried to find the orange again.

"Couldn't have said it better myself."

There was no way Hildy could freeze the hundred or so honey badgers that climbed out of the back of the trucks and I had no idea if I could pop that many. Where was the leader and where was my mother?

Did we have it wrong? Was she not as evil and horrible as I'd assumed? Maybe she had no part in this. Maybe she had become kind and loving.

Did the badgers already have the syringe and were even now coming after me? Was this simply a revenge plot?

Did everyone want to be a fucking Baba Yaga?

Shitshitshitshitshit.

At least five minutes had passed as the badgers lined up and looked as if they were awaiting instruction. They needed to hurry up and show their hand before Mac and I became visible again.

And then she arrived.

My stomach roiled and my chin dropped to my chest as tears filled my eyes. A very expensive Mercedes sedan pulled up and came to a halt in front of the trucks. Two people, and I use the term loosely, as well as a badger stepped out.

She was as beautiful as I remembered and clearly just as heartless. All my instincts screamed to run and try to hug her, but I stayed put. Her boyfriend was the typical vamp—good looking, pale, tall and skinny. His eyes glowed an eerie red and I had to swallow my gasp. He was a scary mother humper. The thought of Mac going up against him didn't leave me with a warm fuzzy feeling. It horrified me.

"Where is it?" my mother snarled.

It was at that moment I realized she had the badger on a chain. He growled and clawed the ground in frustration as she kicked him in the head.

"Kitchen," he hissed. "Behind the fridge."

Mac's body tensed and he silently moved toward the house. Hildy hovered over my mother who clearly didn't see her.

Oh. My. Hell. The syringe and the solution had been in my house the entire time? Why hadn't I considered that possibility? Hide it in the place we were least expected to look.

"Go get it," she snapped. "Hugo darling, go with him. I don't trust the little bastard considering he tried to take the magic for himself the first time."

Well that answered the question as to if she'd been behind it all.

113

ROBYN PETERMAN

"What if we come upon your daughter?" he asked. His voice was as slimy as he was.

"Kill her," she said with a laugh. "No! Wait. Keep her alive. I need her to get the damn magic."

My tears flowed freely now. How could a mother hate her own daughter? Was I doomed to end up like her?

My decision to leave was only solidified by hearing my own mother plan my death. She was so power hungry, it made me ill. Mac wanted and deserved children. If I ended up like her, I was obviously not mother material.

I could feel the invisibility spell slowly wearing off. That was fine. I wanted her to see me before I destroyed her. I wanted her to know it was me.

"What about Shifters?" Hugo inquired as he gnashed his teeth and licked his lips.

"Kill them. I don't want any trail," my mother said viciously.

"I shall drain them. I'm quite hungry, Cassandra," he purred.

"As you wish," she said in a bored tone.

So she was now Cassandra. Whatever. Her name made little difference. A new name didn't change the person.

I became corporeal, but she didn't see me. She was too busy fixing her make up. However, the badgers saw me, and began to hiss and growl.

"Shut up," my mother shouted. "I can end you with a flick of my fingers."

She was wrong. Unless she'd gained a bunch of magic after she'd left, she was capable of very little—a major source of her frustration.

Let's just see if I couldn't add to her frustration.

I started with the honey badger on the end, the one foaming at the mouth and giving me the death stare. Sadly, it was easy. I pointed and he popped. I hated what I had just done, but I knew in the end it was them or me.

My mother jumped and whipped around. Her eyes narrowed dangerously when she finally saw me. It made my heart hurt, but I expected no less.

"Zelda dear," she sneered. "How lovely to see you."

"Nope, can't say it is. You're trespassing," I said coldly.

"Why, I've just come to visit my daughter. Is that such a crime?" she asked with a pout.

I stopped for a minute and reverted back to being ten. I almost asked her if she needed any healing or if there was anything I could do to make her happy. I bit down hard on my cheek to stop myself from trying to placate her and make her

114

love me. It amazed and saddened me to realize I'd fallen for that pout all my life, but not today. And never again.

"Well, it kind of is a crime. I didn't bake a cake. If I knew you were coming, I'd have baked a cake."

The bushes and tree line snickered and it was all I could do to bite back my grin.

Mother glanced around. "Did you hear something?"

"No," I said with a shrug. "Must be your pets."

"Cassandra dear, I completely forgot. I have to be invited into the house. Can you arrange that?" Hugo called out.

"No, she can't," I yelled back. "I don't let dead people in my abode. Too gross."

His hiss made the hair on my arms stand up and my mother's shrill laugh went all through me. She was batshit crazy and her boy-toy wasn't far behind.

"No worries," he snarled. "I'll try the back. I can usually get in that way without an invite."

"Good luck," I called out and then swallowed the 'fuck-face' I wanted to tack onto the end of my sentence. It couldn't be a good idea to rile up a vamp.

Out of the corner of my eye, I saw Mac in his wolf from silently follow the vamp around the house. I prayed quickly to the Goddess to keep him safe. If anything happened to him, I would bite the head off the vamp myself. I didn't care what it would do to me.

"I've just come by because Hildy has something of mine and I wanted to get it back," my mother said in a pathetic attempt at a sweet voice.

"Hildy's dead."

"Oh, is she?" My mother feigned sorrow and I almost laughed. "How terribly sad."

"It is, isn't it? She was murdered," I added and watched her face.

"Oh, how awful. Did they find the murderer?"

"Yep, the little rubbery motherfucker is in my house as we speak."

Zelda," she snapped and shuddered. "There is no reason for such language. I raised you far better than that. Vulgar language is for classless people."

"Well, shitmotherhumperfuckpigbastarddicknosewankertitty," I said with a polite smile.

"Zelda," she ground out, completely appalled and furious now. "Don't make me smite you. And don't think I won't."

"You *really* don't want to fuck with me," I said as my people began to emerge from the bushes and trees.

She glanced around alarmed, caught by surprise and then gave me a small evil smile.

"Kill them," she shouted to her honey badger army. "Leave no one alive except her." She pointed to me and then stepped away from the fray.

She was such a fucking wussy. I was so not like her.

I was like the insane warlock who was in the basement most likely cheating at poker with Baba Yaga's crew of gnomes.

I was like my ghost of an aunt who had the power to heal.

But mostly I was me—just me. I was a slightly less selfish, still unstable, and somewhat dangerous witch who had friends, a real home, and three fat cats. I had a wolf who thought he was in love with me. Me, the unlovable girl. I had things to live for and I'd be damned if I was going to let that woman take any of it away today. I had already lost my childhood to her, but I would not lose my current life.

"Attack," I shouted as I sent a thread of magic which pinned my mother against the car.

Trapping her trapped her magic and she couldn't hurt anyone. The Shifters fought like the animals they were and gave the badgers an ugly run for their money. I ran to the house to find the honey badger leader before he found the syringe. It had to be destroyed.

Before I hit the porch, the badger emerged looking confused and enraged. "It's gone," he screamed above the melee. "It's not there."

His voice boomed over the battle and my mother's shriek made my blood curdle.

Where in the hell was it?

My mother broke free of my magical ropes and hurled a fireball at my head narrowly missing. Shit, it looked like mommy dearest had gained some power since I last saw her. Not good. Not good at all.

"If I can't have your magic, neither can you," she screamed like a banshee at causing me to slap my hands over my ears.

And that's when all hell broke loose.

Chapter 17

I glanced around wildly to see how my people were faring. They were holding up far better than the honey badgers even though we were out numbered. Chuck fought closest to the porch. He was a freakin' killing machine. He even scared me and we were on the same team.

"Oh shit," he grunted as he slammed two badger's heads together and knocked them unconscious. "What did this syringe look like?"

"Um... it's like the thing the doctor uses when he gives you a shot but bigger," I ground out as I popped three badgers who clearly had my name on their list of things to kill.

"I don't go to a doctor. I go to the Shifter Wanker. Does it look kind of like a meat baster with a pointy needle on the end?"

"It could be described that way," I said as I ducked a flying badger DeeDee had bucked across the yard and searched for my mother. Where had she gone?

"Was it filled with blue goopy stuff?" he inquired as he tore the head of another rubbery bastard and threw it at several others.

"Yep," I said.

"Dude, remember I told you I made a mess when I fixed the fridge?"

"Yep," I answered starting to feel giddy.

"I busted the thing to smithereens. Cleaned it up and threw it out in the garbage," he said with a shit-eating grin on his bear face. "It was toast. Completely unrecognizable as anything but dust."

"Yesssssssss," I hissed in triumph as I zapped several badgers headed for Roger and Simon. "Chuck I think I love you!"

"Love you more, little witch," he grunted and went back to killing shit.

The battle was getting uglier and I was losing people. Badger popsicles littered the lawn. Hildy had frozen at least ten and was looking weak and more transparent. Damn it, I needed Mac, but he was with the vamp. Please, please, please let him be okay.

This had been going well. The syringe was gone as well as the solution. The tools of the lurking fucking evil had been eliminated. Problem was that part of the lurking fucking evil was still in my front yard. My job was to protect my people. Where in the hell was the orange magic Hildy mentioned? I knew if I could summon it I could end the fighting.

I didn't think it could get any clusterfuckier, but I was wrong—very wrong.

Mac and the vampire were entwined like lovers in a death grip and flew like a cannonball being shot off into the front yard. I had no clue who was winning and my heart lodged in my throat. Chuck's roar pulled me away from the horror of Mac and Hugo.

The badgers had clearly gotten a second wind and were advancing like bats out of hell. They were winning. Fucking unacceptable.

My fury consumed me and my entire body lit up like a Christmas tree on fire. With my arms over my head I chanted like I'd never chanted before. A wind mixed with the blood of the dead lying in my yard whipped up and swirled violently through the battle. The sound was deafening and my insides burned like a furnace.

Dropping to my knees, I started to chant. My pain was nothing compared to the wounded and fallen. I was still here and I could make a difference to the ones who lived. I would. I believed in myself. I still hadn't found the orange, but what I had found inside me might just be enough.

The magical tornado blasted across the lawn, lifting the remaining badgers and tearing them to shreds. The bile in my stomach rose to my throat, but I kept chanting. The lives of my people were at stake and I could stop the madness. I had to stop the madness. It was my fate.

The Shifters froze and watched me cause the destruction of the enemy with both admiration and fear. I'd have done the same in their shoes. I prayed they'd still like me after they'd seen the havoc I could wreak.

I hoped I could live with myself...

Then it ended.

It was over. Every single badger was dead.

The clapping took me by surprise and the kneeling was a shock.

"Whisperer, whisperer, whisperer," they chanted.

I scanned the yard frantically for Mac. He stood apart from the crowd in his wolf form with the head of the vampire in his teeth. He was torn up and bleeding, but he was alive. I tried to breathe a huge sigh of relief, but the vise like hold around my neck prohibited me.

"Come a step closer and I kill her," my mother hissed, completely unhinged.

Her face was over my right shoulder and I knew she could see the detached head of her lover now lying at my wolf's feet. Her body trembled as she shot small knife like daggers of magic into my back. The pain was intense, but the lack of breathing was more of a problem at the moment.

I prayed to the Goddess for Hildy's help, but she lay on the ground barely visible only feet away. If my mother succeeded in killing me, I knew she wouldn't make it out alive. She was far too out numbered even with her magic.

But if I was going down, she was coming with me.

Where in the fuck was the orange?

"Here's how this will work," she barked as she tightened her grasp on my neck. "I'm going to take a little drive with my daughter and no one is going to stop me. If you do, she dies."

"And if we don't, she dies," Chuck growled. "I really don't see that as a fair option, lady."

"Shut up," she snarled and zapped me with a volt that made me convulse and see stars.

She was fucking serious and her grip blocked my magic. She had clearly been studying with someone.

"Don't underestimate stupidity," Fat Bastard croaked as he and the other two cats waddled into the clearing.

They looked like shit on a stick, but thankfully they were alive. Jango was missing most of his fur and Boba seemed to be sporting a few less teeth. However the advice was outstanding.

I lifted my foot and came down on her instep with a vengeance, causing her grip to loosen for a brief second. It was all I needed.

"Everyone back up," I commanded. "She's mine."

As she hopped around and regained her balance, I shoved her away. It was time for a witch smack down. I only hoped Simon would be able to keep his butt shut. I didn't need to throw up during a crucial moment.

"May the best witch win," my mother sneered with wild eyes as she hurled a blue fireball at my head, missing me but setting the porch on fire.

Goddess, she really wanted to kill me. A secret part of my heart that I had kept for her finally died. I could no longer pretend she would change. I needed to defend myself and stop her from her megalomaniac quest.

I countered with an explosion that singed off most of her hair. My stupid misplaced allegiance kept me from going for kill spots or popping her. Her demented wail of fury went straight to my toes as I wondered just how strong she was.

Blast after blast and zap after zap were traded. I was burned and bleeding, but I was still standing. The Shifters took me at my word and had backed away. Mac stood at the front of the group and looked ready to blow a gasket. This was my fight, not his or theirs. Mac's respect for me was humbling.

The porch was now in flames and I felt the blazing heat at my back.

"Is there anyone in the house?" she demanded as she raised her hands and aimed.

Wanda, Bo, Daaaaad, Sassy, older Shifters, the children and the warlocks were in my house. The look of horror on my face answered her question and she winked.

Time slowed and I raised my hands to deflect her fireball with my own magic, but I was too slow. It was enormous and flew from her hands as she shrieked like a wounded animal. I watched in shock as it headed toward the house to incinerate it and I screamed.

I was knocked to the ground as a huge mass dove through the air and took the brunt of her evil magic in his chest. Hildy's weak moan confirmed it was Chuck. He was on fire and I couldn't even see his body through the flames.

But that didn't satisfy my mother. She threw another as I crawled to my feet and the house exploded behind me.

I swung to gape at it in shock. Flames licked hundreds of feet into the sky. The inferno that had been my home mocked me. I didn't belong anywhere now. She'd taken my father and she'd taken my home.

The sound that left my mouth was inhuman. With Chuck dying a foot away from me and my dad and friends burning to death in my basement, I found the orange—or maybe it found me.

My vision blurred and my skin grew hot. The orange magic rose up inside me with a frightening rage I'd never know. I was no longer just a witch who healed. I was a fucking magical maniac who was able to fly without a broom.

I dove for my mother like a bullet flying out of a gun and gut punched her with my head, flinging her across the lawn. But that was just the appetizer.

Again I flew and landed a non-magical punch to her face that broke her lovely nose. I winced as blood spurted all over the two of us. She had destroyed my life, killed my friend and murdered my father. She would die by my hand in honor of my dad.

My tears almost blinded me. I hated what I was doing, but I couldn't stop.

"Die bitch," she hissed as she pulled up her magic and threw me off of her. "I was meant to rule, not you."

The wave of magic she threw was painful, but I was beyond feeling it. I never even got to call Naked Dude, Dad. He wanted me to call him Dad. I screwed that up too. The panic inside me was so real my breathing came in short uneven spurts. Spots danced in front of my eyes and I simply wanted to curl up in a ball and block out the world.

"I never should have had you," she screeched and laughed. It was a brittle sound and so very cruel. "You're worthless."

Energy from a place deeply hidden inside me burst free. I flew at her again, knocking her to the ground with a sickening thud. I had her exactly where I wanted her. She was helpless and I pinned her down with both my hands and my magic. It would be within my rights as a witch to kill her, but I couldn't. She killed my friends and my father. She wanted me dead and I still couldn't do it. I was a healer not a killer. I already had so much blood on my hands I was unsure how I would fare after all was said and done.

"You can't do it," she hissed and spat at me.

"You're right, I can't," I said as I wiped her spit from my cheek. I propped her still magically trapped body into a sitting position under a tree.

"You're weak," she said with disgusted snort. "You'll never be a Baba Yaga."

All she ever really wanted was power—absolute power and nothing else. She didn't want me or my father or any kind of love. She was incapable of feeling anything at all. Absolute power corrupts absolutely. In that moment, I realized I didn't have to kill her physically to kill her.

"I don't want to be a Baba Yaga," I told her. "Never even aspired to that."

I didn't bother to add I'd only realized it was merely a title this morning...

I straddled her legs and kissed her gently on her forehead head. "I love you even though you don't love me. You're right. I can't kill you. However, it's not because I can't. It's because I won't. I wasn't made that way. But what I can do to you is far worse."

"Stupid girl, get off of me and let me go. I knew you'd amount to nothing."

"That's where you're wrong, mother. I am something. I'm something *wonderful*."

Her eyes grew wide with terror as I reared back my fist and aimed at her chest.

"No!" she wailed, but it was too late to bargain. The store was closed.

The feeling of my fist deep in her chest was horrifying. It was squishy and bloody, but I knew what I was searching for. It came to me quickly—I was thankful for that. I didn't want it, but she was no longer allowed to have it. She'd lost her right.

Her power floated to my hand, crawled up my arm and entered my body. I shuddered as I realized it was laced with black magic. Fuck. I now had my own magic, my aunt's and my mother's dark shit. This was surely a very bad thing, but what else was there to do?

I stood on shaky legs and stepped away. I was tired. I was done. She was bad and had worn out her welcome.

With a flick of my hand, I closed the gaping wound I'd made in her chest. My mother would live, but she would live as a mortal. It was a destiny worse than death for any witch.

I didn't kill her, but actually I had. That's when I threw up.

And after that little display of gross, I fell to my knees and sobbed.

Chapter 18

Mac's strong arms engulfed me and I found myself surrounded by Shifters. Tears clouded my vision, but I felt safe for a moment.

And then I remembered... Dad and Chuck and Wanda and Bo and Sassy. Gone. My sobbing renewed and I knew my heartbreak would last for eternity.

I'd only found my father a little over a month ago. It wasn't fair that he was taken from me so soon. Was it me? Was it my fault somehow? The panic bubbled up inside me and I buried my head in Mac's chest.

"I need gum," I whispered brokenly.

"What, baby?" he asked as he raised my chin.

I quickly pulled away. My breath could kill. Throw up breath was not something I wanted to share.

"Here you go," Roger said as he handed me five pieces.

I nodded my thanks. He looked bad, but he was still here.

"How many did we lose?" I asked and closed my eyes.

"Fifteen," DeeDee said gravely. "And Chuck."

I was silent as I digested this. Had no one died in the battle? There had to be at least fifteen in the basement not counting the warlocks. I idly wondered if the Baba Yaga would be angry about her posse being blown up.

I began to cough the smoke up from my lungs and couldn't stop. Mac loosened his hold and rubbed my back.

"Get her some water," he instructed.

"The kind from the toilet or the sink?" Sassy asked.

"Oh my hell... from the sink," I choked out between coughs.

"The toilet is better," she informed me clearly in the know. "It's colder and has sparkly stuff in it."

"I do not drink from...Wait," I croaked as I whipped my head around. "You're dead."

"Now that's just rude," Sassy said with a huge smile. "I mean I might be dead later when you see what accidentally happened to your Prada boots. Oh snap...I'm sorry, but they blew up. Why did I tattle on myself? I'm such a doucheweasel."

"You're supposed to be dead," I stuttered as a sob burst from my lips. "The house—the fire—the basement."

I was choking and crying. There was no way she could have lived through the blast and fire, unless she'd left the basement. Had they all left the basement? Please, please, please...

"The fire. It didn't kill you?" I asked, terrified to ask about the others.

"Hell no, those little warlock fuckers conjured up some kind of impenetrable explosion proof bubble and we all got under it."

"Them bastards saved your life," Jango Fett said with admiration for the same little dudes who had tried to burn him alive yesterday.

"All?" I whispered hopefully.

"Yes, all," my dad said as he broke through the crowd of concerned Shifters. He lifted me from Mac's arms and held me tight.

My body shook violently and my crying reached what could politely be called snotty hysteria.

"I love you, Dad," I blubbered. "I will call you Dad everyday for the rest of my years. I promise. No more Daaaaad, Nadudio, Naked Dude, Dudio or Fabio—just Dad."

"I love you too," he whispered against my hair. "And I don't care what you call me as long as you love me."

"I took her magic," I told him and waited for his reaction.

"You were kind," he said with steel in his voice as he stared at the passed out body of my mother with hatred. "I would have tortured her for hours and then killed her."

"I couldn't do it. I'm not made that way."

"You actually did something far worse than death," Baba Yaga sang as she poofed in along with a burst of rainbow glitter.

"You," I hissed as I disengaged from my dad and marched over to her. "You are a real assmonkey, Carol."

The gasps from the peanut gallery were loud and alarmed. I didn't care. Baba Yopoopy was on my shit list.

"Hello to you too," she said with a grin as she adjusted her silver unitard and fluffed her hot pink fuzzy leg warmers.

Her outfit threw me for a loop, but I was on a fucking

mission. However, the fashion talk was coming soon—especially if she was going to date my dad.

"Some of my people died today. What the hell were you thinking by leaving?" I demanded all up in her face.

"I left you to your fate, dear child," she said with slightly narrowed eyes. "And you learned my name how?"

"Fate," I snapped. "It was my fate to know your name, Carol."

"I suppose you're right," she said and sighed dramatically. "You completed your mission... as did you, Sassy."

"I'm not going anywhere else, Carol. No more dumbass screw ball missions for me," Sassy threatened. "I like it here and I'm staying. Jeeves is hot and likes horses. Zelda's house rocks...Whoops, I mean rocked."

We all turned and took in the still smoldering pile of ash that used to be my beautiful home. There was a lump in my throat, but I didn't cry. The house was simply a house. People mattered, not stuff. Holy hell, I was growing up.

"And Chuck died nobly," Baba Yaga said with a delighted smile as she clapped her hands.

That was fucking *it*.

I didn't care if she was the leader of all witches. She was crazy and cruel. How could she be joyous over the death of my friend?

"What the hell is wrong with you," I shouted. "Chuck was my friend. I loved him."

"You certainly love a lot of people now," she commented with raised eyebrows.

"Figure of speech," I mumbled as her tinkling giggle made me grind my teeth.

I was pretty sure I did love all these people and I was beginning to believe that they loved me too.

"Chuck is happy," she said softly. "Turn around and see for yourself."

Slowly I turned and gasped as tears filled my eyes for the umpteenth time today. Chuck and Hildy floated together hand in hand. Their love was so evident it made me cry harder.

"To be without your mate is a slow death," Baba said as she walked toward her Hildy and Chuck. "You died nobly my friend. You both have the Goddess's blessing to go on to the Next Adventure. I will miss you so."

"Wait," I cried out as I ran over to my aunt and my friend. "I don't want you to go. I want you to stay."

"Oh my dear beautiful child," Hildy said as she floated down to me. "This is no longer my world. I have done all I was supposed to do and now it's time for us to go. You are ready. You are strong. I love you more than you will ever know."

"But I want you with me," I whispered.

"That is not what fate decrees," she said sadly. "Fate and the Goddess smiled on us letting me come back and meet you. It makes my life complete. You were magnificent and you will be fine."

"Can you visit?" I implored.

Hildy looked to Chuck and then back at me. "I don't think so, but I will be your Guardian Angel. I will always watch over you. You must believe that."

"I don't want you to be my Guardian Angel," I said. "I want you with me. Who's going to teach me to use the stupid orange magic?"

"Dear, I've never actually pulled it up. Seeing you use it was a first for me too," she said with a giggle.

"Are you shitting me?" I demanded.

"Do I look like I'm shitting you?" she replied with a smirk.

"Might have been nice to have shared that little piece of info with me," I said as I gave her my raised eyebrow look.

"You had a lot on your plate, sweetie. Didn't want to freak you out," she said with a shrug and a grin.

She floated back to Chuck and he happily wrapped her in his strong transparent arms. They were beautiful together. My dad walked to his sister and flipped her the bird as tears streamed down his face.

"I love you, jackass," he said softly as he blew his sister a kiss.

"Back at ya, doucheknocker," she said as she flipped him off with a sweet smile.

"Are you sure about this?" I asked one more time, praying they'd stay with me.

"It's our time. No one lives forever. The Next Adventure is where Chuck and I are supposed to be now. Wish us well and release us."

"I'll miss you, little witch," Chuck said with a wink. "And my pick up truck is yours. You can get rid of your piece of shit lime green Kia. Please let us go now."

"You got a lime green one?" Sassy huffed jealously. "My piece of crap was purple. How is that fair?

"You can have mine," I told her.

"Yessssssssssssss," she said and slapped Jeeves a high five.

"It's time for them to go, Zelda," Baba Yaga urged me.

Wait. What? I had to sign off on this to let them go? My gaze shot to Baba Yaga who watched me intensely. Her nod was quick and curt. She turned her back and walked away. I realized in that moment I could make them stay with me. I knew I could make them happy here.

Hildy had Chuck now. We could rebuild the house and all live together.

All eyes were on me. Shit.

"Why is it my call?" I asked.

"Because you're the healer. You are the Shifter Whisperer," Chuck replied simply.

"Shifter Wanker," I corrected him with a smile.

"Right," he nodded and chuckled. "We're caught here and we need someone with strong magic and healing power to lead us back to the Goddess."

What I wanted to do was wrong. What I was going to do would shred me. I looked to the sky and closed my eyes. I took a deep breath and pulled up my big girl panties. I was going to let them go. It was right and would be my final gift to them. I blew my beloved aunt and dear friend a kiss and I reached down deep.

Raising my arms to the stars, I felt a calming lavender magic flow through me. It was powerful and warm. It was something new to me and it was good.

"Goddess of life and death, please heed my prayer
With your sacred light and exquisite care
Take these two that I love into your heart
Find the Next Adventure and a blessed new start"

A cool, ocean scented breeze blew up and tiny orbs of sparkling light rained down from above. The Shifters were as mesmerized as I. The gorgeous bubbles surrounded Hildy and Chuck and I got a momentary peek at pure peace. Their faces transformed to something so very beautiful, it felt wrong to look at it. The blissful joy was so comforting my tears fell yet again.

It was right, I felt foolish now for my desire to make them stay. Fate knew what she was doing and apparently so did the Goddess. Now if only I could get that smart.

Slowly Hildy and Chuck became one with the glittering orbs and began to float away. I reached up and touched one. It was warm and soft. It bounced off my fingers and brushed my cheek. The feeling was one I would never forget and I hoped that Hildy and Chuck were feeling the same thing.

"They are," Baba Yaga whispered as she put her arm around me. "Only much, much better."

I decided not to broach the sticky subject that she had

127

obviously read my mind and just stuck to watching the bubbles fade to black. I didn't feel the need to cry. I wanted to sing with joy but I didn't. My tone deaf warbling would have destroyed the precious moment.

"I was sure you'd say 'fuck' somewhere in that spell," Fat Bastard commented as he wound his fat carcass around my legs.

"Yeah well, it didn't rhyme. If it had, I promise I would have used it," I said.

"Good enough for me," he grunted.

"Where are my boys?" Baba Yaga yelled.

The warlocks slithered in to the clearing and clumped together right in front of me.

"We're slightly sorry for trying to incinerate you and yours yesterday," the ugliest of the group said with great reluctance as the other bobble heads nodded in agreement. "We will not do it again."

"Damn right, you won't," Mac growled as he took his place at my side. He took my bruised and still bleeding hand gently in his.

"You owe me half a mil," Fat Bastard told the warlocks as he sharpened his kitty claws.

Jango and Boba were too busy grooming their nads to back their partner up, but it was unnecessary. The warlock pulled out a checkbook and grudgingly wrote out a check.

"While you have that out, I'll take my three million," Dad said as he sheepishly grinned at me. "What? I have to buy you all new clothes!"

I rolled my eyes and laughed. My Dad was a piece of work and I was so happy he was mine. It never would have worked between us if he was normal.

"Are those checks any good?" I asked.

"Yes," Baba Yaga said. "My boys are loaded, but shitty poker players. I've warned them time and time again about this very thing."

"They cheat," one of the warlocks groused.

"Can you prove it?" Dad inquired with an evil little grin.

The warlock turned an unbecoming shade of red and stayed silent.

"I like your dad," Fat Bastard said. Then he over-extended his back leg and joined his cohorts in the ball-licking contest they were obviously having.

"Me too," I agreed. "Me too."

With a grand wave of his hand, my dad made all of the carnage disappear except for the fallen Shifters. Wanda, Simon, DeeDee and Roger, with great care and respect, began to retrieve their bodies. We watched in silence until they had gently covered all the dead and laid them in one of the military vehicles the badgers had used.

It tore at me that it was too late to save them, but there were still many injured I needed to attend to.

"If you're hurt, please line up," I instructed. "I'm kind of running low here so those with the worst wounds need to go first."

I worked quickly and efficiently as I healed my friends and neighbors. It was painful and it sucked wads, but I was so grateful to be able to do it. I even healed Sassy who gaped at me with wonder.

"That was fucking cool," she gushed as the burns on her arms disappeared. "Why can't I do something like that?"

"Because you blow things up and dig through gray matter," I told her as I flopped down on the ground in exhaustion.

"Don't forget fornicating," Jango added.

"She's quite wonderful at that," Jeeves chimed in and then blushed like a tomato. "Dad?" he asked Mac.

"Yes?" Mac replied warily.

"I was wondering if it would be okay for Sassy to spend the night for a few months since she doesn't have a house anymore."

"Um…" Mac was at a total loss for words and quite honestly so was I.

I didn't have a house either. Where were Dad and I supposed to go? I couldn't move in with Mac. That would complicate matters to clusterfuck levels. I was still going to leave.

"We will camp out for a few days until I can find some warlocks who specialize in construction," Dad cut in before Mac insisted we come with him.

"Witches specialize in construction?" I asked, surprised yet again about how much I didn't know.

"He's making that up," Baba Yoknowitall said with a laugh as she slapped my Dad's ass. "I can rebuild your house right now."

I gulped and wondered if it would be an 80's wonderland, but beggars couldn't be choosers.

"Fix it, please," I said as Mac huffed his displeasure.

With a frightening back flip and a couple of chants that sounded like fornicating cats, Carol the Baba Yaga, rebuilt my house. The mirror balls in every room were evident from the yard and I sighed in defeat.

"Boys, get the newly turned mortal and bring her with us. I have a few choice words for her when she wakes up," Baba Yaga said as the warlocks obeyed her. "Fabio, I'll see you on Tuesday. Wear the yoga pants."

On that gag-inducing note, she and her cronies poofed away in a cloud of crouch smoke.

"I say we call it a night," Dad advised as he wandered up to the house to hit the hay.

The cats followed behind and the Shifters all thanked me before they made their way home. I sighed and ran my hands through my tangled hair. Goddess, I must look like hell.

"You're beautiful," Mac said reverently.

"You're in my head," I accused with another sigh.

"Yep," he agreed and began to massage my shoulders. "We need to talk."

Oh shit.

Chapter 19

"I'm kind of tired," I said, wanting to avoid everything and anything he had to say.

"Too bad," he shot back as he led me to the backyard and arranged us on a chaise by the pool.

The area was ransacked. Most everything I'd conjured up had been destroyed.

"Was it hard to kill the vampire?" I asked as I let my body relax against his.

"I didn't want to kill him, but he gave me no choice," he said, playing with my hair.

"How so?"

"I offered him an out if he talked, but he insisted he was hungry and went for my neck. So I went for his head. I won. He lost. End of story."

I knew there was much more to the tale, but the details might be too much to handle after this evening's activities. I'd make him tell me tomorrow before I'd eaten. I expected it to be gag worthy.

"I'm hungry," I said, trying to put off the inevitable.

"You're always hungry," he commented as he lifted me up and turned me to face him. "You're not leaving, Zelda."

"You're not the boss of me," I informed him.

"True," he said. "And you're not a coward."

"Maybe I am," I countered.

He sighed and ran his hands through his hair. "Why? Why are you so afraid of what's happening between us?"

I got up and began to pace. His nearness clouded my

judgment and I needed to think straight.

"You saw my mother," I snapped.

"Yes. And?"

"Apples don't fall far from trees, Mac. You want puppies. I can't have puppies," I said in exasperation as my pacing sped up.

"We'd have babies, Zelda."

"Babies. Puppies. It doesn't matter. I'm not mother material. How do we know I wouldn't want to kill them?" I demanded shrilly.

Mac's laugh made me want to smack him. He didn't get it at all.

"Your tree also includes Hildy and your father. They are loving and good," he said calmly.

"I wasn't raised by them. I was raised by the monster I made mortal tonight. That's the problem. I'm not lovable. I don't know how to love," I insisted, trying to make him see what a mistake I was.

"I beg to differ," he said. "And you can't leave. We have a contract."

"What?" I asked. He was nuts. "What contract?"

"Eight more dates. I get eight more dates," he said with narrowed eyes that turned me on like a switch.

"Oh my Goddess," I yelled. "You have got to be kidding me. After all we went through today, you'd hold me to those stupid dates?"

"Yep," he said with a sexy smirk. "I most certainly will. If after eight more dates you want to leave, you're free to go. But I promise you, you'll want to stay."

"You're that cocky?" I asked as I stopped my pacing and gaped at him.

"Nope, I'm that good."

I couldn't hold back my laughter. He was an arrogant ass and I adored him. He knew he had me when he challenged my word. A witch was only as good as her word and I'd made the damn deal in the first place.

But even if he'd won the battle today, sadly I knew I'd win the war. Even eight more dates couldn't change my past. I was what I was and he deserved more. It would be even harder to leave when the dates were done, but I was growing up. I no longer came first.

"Okay," I said. "Eight more dates, but that's all."

"Whatever you say, baby," he replied as he scooped me up and marched us to the house.

I couldn't say no. I didn't want to say no.

I was exactly where I wanted to be.

Epilogue

I couldn't believe how professional the office looked. I expected something run down and seedy—just like his hobby. I was ten minutes early and was beyond pissed off at myself for being here. What kind of idiot was I? A big one. I'd lost a damn hand of poker to Dad and this was my payment.

I was never playing poker with him again. The warlocks had been correct—he cheated.

My Dad was a dick.

"Doctor Roger will see you now," a cute fox Shifter named Susan told me in a professional tone.

I snickered at the title and Susan gave me an odd look. I swallowed back all the snarky comments that were on the tip of my tongue and followed her back. I was going to shrink all of my Dad's clothes and shoes when I got home. The thought made me happy.

"Welcome, Zelda. Good to see you," Roger said from behind a huge desk. He was clearly making up for his inadequacies.

I waited for Susan to leave and then I laid it out.

"I lost a bet. That's why I'm here. I do not want to be here—at all. If you look a below my neck, I will punch you in the head. Clear?"

"Um... yes," Roger said somewhat alarmed, but staring straight at my face.

"Good. I definitely need my head shrunk, but I just can't take you seriously," I explained. "I figured we could just chat about things other than my mental wellbeing while I'm here."

"Exactly how many times will you be here?" Roger inquired

as diplomatically as he could.

"Nine," I ground out wanting to smite my Dad to hell. "Since you do them in hours, I figure we can do three a day for three days and I'll have paid my debt."

"I have to be with you three hours a day for three days straight?" Roger choked out, clearly terrified.

"Yes. Do you have a problem with it?" I asked with narrowed eyes.

"No, no. Not at all," he said shakily.

Damn it, I was starting to feel bad. I'd clearly scared the hell out of him. He didn't deserve the ire that was directed at my Dad. Poor Roger was just a porno-addicted therapist—not the enemy.

"Look, I'm sorry. We might have gotten off to a bad start here," I conceded.

"Ya think?" Roger asked with an eye roll.

"Therapists are not supposed to roll their eyes," I told him with an eye roll of my own.

"I didn't think I was actually your therapist," he logically answered.

"You're not," I huffed.

The silence got kind of boring as we both pretended to be absorbed in the office decor.

"So, ahhhh… what would you like to chat about?" Roger inquired politely.

I had to be here. I was going to spend nine hours with the rabbit over the next three days. Everyone swore he was a good therapist. What the fuck did I have to lose?

"Um… how about my mom?" I suggested and then punched myself in the head.

"I think that's a very good place to start," Roger said warmly as he pulled out a pad of paper and got comfortable. "Go ahead, Zelda."

With a huge put upon sigh, I did. Would it help? I doubted it, but again… I had nothing to lose. Eight more dates with Mac and I was blowing this town.

Maybe…

The End (for now) # #

Note From the Author

: If you enjoyed this ebook, please consider leaving a positive review or rating on the site where you purchased it. Reader reviews help my books continue to be valued by distributors/resellers and help new readers make decisions about reading them. You are the reason I write these stories and I sincerely appreciate you!

Many thanks for your support,
~ Robyn Peterman

Visit me on my website at http://www.robynpeterman.com.

Excerpt from *Fashionably Hotter Than Hell*

Book Five of THE HOT DAMNED Series

BOOK FIVE
THE HOT DAMNED SERIES

Fashionably
HOTTER
THAN HELL

NEW YORK TIMES AND USA TODAY BESTSELLING AUTHOR
ROBYN PETERMAN

Book Description

What does a Vampyre do when the woman he's chased for two hundred years is still trying to get away? He plays dirty.

Welcome to my own personal Hell.

Where life is steamy and the sex is sizzling.

Only I would be blessed with a Vampyre mate that I'd have to chase for two centuries.

Now to my great dismay, I have competition for her very existence—not for her hand, for her life.

Name: Heathcliff.

Occupation: Vampyre Warrior—one of the deadliest in the world.

I plan. I fight. I win.

Always.

It's just never taken this damned long.

Raquel may run and she may hide, but she is mine and I will no longer accept no for an answer. We were made for each other and nothing will change that simple fact... except maybe the Trolls or the Wraiths or the recluse Vampyre that wants to drink my mate dry.

Damn it, I thought the chase was difficult... keeping Raquel alive might prove to be my undoing.

Chapter 1

"If you tell anyone, I will deny it and decapitate you," she said casually as she pulled her panties on.

"Noted," I replied as I watched her through hooded lids and pondered what it would take to get her to remove the offending scrap of material and go for another round. Was I insane? Yes. Did I have a death wish? Absolutely.

"I just said I would remove your head and that's all you have to say?" she demanded.

"Depends on which head you're talking about."

"Oh my God. You're disgusting," she yelled as she hurled a lamp at my way.

Ducking the light fixture, I rolled off the bed and donned my jeans. I winked as I caught her ogling my backside. "I heard you and I raise you one. I will deflower, deny, and decapitate. Damn." I shook my head sadly while grinning from ear to ear. "Already deflowered...two hundred years ago."

"You're an ass," she hissed as she yanked on the rest of her clothes, covering a body that was made for sin.

However, the mouth left much to be desired. Well, not when it was wrapped around my...

"This was a mistake and will not be repeated," she informed me haughtily as she twisted her red curls into some kind of sexy looking bird's nest on the top of her head. "Never going to happen again."

I shrugged and grinned. Who was she trying to convince? Herself? Me? We'd been playing this game for quite a while. I was tempted to make a wager with her due to the fact she had a hard time passing up a bet or a dare, but that could backfire on me in an enormous way.

"Heard that one before, Red." I slid my shirt over my head and quickly sidestepped a left hook from the insane woman I'd just given eight consecutive orgasms to.

"My name is not *Red*. If you value your jewels you'll remember that," she snapped as she strapped a dagger to the sexiest thigh I'd ever seen.

Why were the hot ones certifiable? I slid my katana into its sheath and waited patiently for the next insult. Was I a glutton for punishment? You bet, but it was worth every damned second.

"You know," she purred, "you're not really that good."

"Interesting," I commented as I slipped a knife into my boot. "That's not what you screamed ten minutes ago."

The look on her face was priceless. The next words from her mouth…not so much.

"I faked it."

Rolling my eyes, I wondered for a sickening moment if that was true and immediately decided it was bullshit. I was over two hundred years old. I knew when a woman faked it. Didn't I?

I shrugged and chuckled. "Well, that's too bad because I enjoyed the Hell out of it. Especially when you screamed my name and your body clamped itself around my…"

"Enough," she shouted as she practically sprinted to the door. "You're an arrogant son of a bitch and I can't stand the sight of you. You will never touch me again. I will no longer slum it with lowlife assholes like you and your big mouth and your big ego and your big…"

"Dick?" I asked politely.

"In your dreams," she informed me over her shoulder as she hightailed it out of my suite like the Devil was on her heels.

I flopped back down on my bed and smiled. Now I *knew* she was lying…

Score one for me.

***

Later that afternoon…

All Hell had broken loose. I hadn't had so much fun in ages. Literally.

The office was in shambles, but I couldn't stop myself. Her anger was as sexy as everything else about her.

"Bet you can't nail my head," I challenged. Riling her up had become my favorite pastime.

"Bet this, jackass," she shouted as she hurled something

colorful and large.

The object flew through the air like a bullet out of a gun. I couldn't even make out what it was.

"Shrew," I shot back with a laugh as I ducked. The crash was loud. I winced as I realized she'd just annihilated an ancient Ming vase.

"Moor dweller," she hissed as she flung another irreplaceable artifact at my head.

"Very clever," I replied as I dodged the incoming projectile.

"I thought so...*Heathcliff*," she purred.

Her smile was infuriating and lamentably hot. The office was decimated. There was very little else to break except for her.

It would be far easier to be in a room with the abomination if I didn't want to kill her or bed her. I was torn between which one would give me more satisfaction—tearing her arm off or losing myself inside of her body. Unfortunately neither was a viable option at the present time. Her fiery red curls had fallen out of the mess on her head and fell loosely down her back. Her creamy skin tempted me to distraction and her scent made me dizzy. She was every man's fantasy and my personal nightmare. Even the sprinkling of freckles across the bridge of her nose, which she usually disguised with glamour were making my pants tight and uncomfortable at the moment.

Working as a team had been a tremendously bad idea, evidenced by the rubble that used to be Prince Ethan's study— my dearest friend and brother to the nightmare that was staring daggers at me from five feet away. Thankfully Ethan's son, young Samuel, our one and only student, had not been present for the latest showdown between his teacher, *her* and his fight coach, *me*.

I'd simply leave the office. That was far more mature than throwing her over my knee and spanking her. Or, God forbid, stripping her down and fucking her into submission on the couch we had destroyed in our melee. Leaving would ensure that she lived another day in her long immortal life and that I wouldn't be brought up on charges for killing a Princess—no matter how much she deserved it.

I stiffly turned to go and was shoved right back into the room by my cousin Astrid, the mother of the child we were supposed to be teaching.

"What in Satan's slightly misguided obsession with Journey happened to this office?" Astrid demanded as she stormed into the room and plopped down on what used to be a priceless antique settee. "Motherfucker, this chair just stabbed me in the ass."

"Ask Wuthering Heights," the flame haired viper snapped as she pointed at me with her middle finger—definitely not an accident on her part.

I glanced up at the ceiling hoping against hope it would give me the strength not to rip an appendage from her body. I'd had enough of the *Wuthering Heights* slams. Yes, I was named after a literary character. And yes, my sister was named Cathy. However, my mother had been friends with Emily Brontë...hence the names. I'd come to terms with it hundreds of years ago—or so I'd thought.

"So Cousin Heathcliff," Astrid said as she grinned at me. "Care to enlighten me?"

"Not particularly," I told her. "Why don't you ask the *lady*?"

My nightmare blushed in fury. Her delicate hands fisted at her sides and her eyes blazed green, which delighted me to no end and made the erection in my pants even more painful. Vampyres didn't blush, but this one did—an anomaly that fascinated me.

"Raquel?" Astrid questioned as her head bobbed back and forth between us like a spectator at a tennis match.

"He has anger issues," Raquel spat.

"Pot, kettle, black," I muttered.

"Plus he keeps daring me," she accused as if it were all my fault.

"Well, that certainly sucks," Astrid said. She gave me the stink eye while acting as if the bullshit Raquel just spouted made sense. "While I find all of that fanfuckingfascinating, do you think you guys could take this outside instead of destroying my house?"

"Ask him," Raquel said without looking at me.

"You're buying this crap from her?" I demanded of my cousin.

Astrid shrugged and grinned.

Raquel completely ignored me and went on. "Anyway, he's a chauvinistic pig who clearly comes from a line of pigs. I can't be expected to work with him."

Astrid was enjoying herself far too much. She found a clutter free spot on the floor and got comfortable. My cousin, too many times removed to remember the number, loved drama—especially drama that she didn't create.

"You do realize you just called me a swine oh sister in law," Astrid announced as Raquel blanched.

No one wanted to incur Astrid's wrath.

My mother had been Astrid's grandmother several hundred years after she had given birth to my sister and me. While at first it had been awkward and alarming since Astrid and I mistakenly thought we were attracted to each other, it turned out to be a blessing. The logistics of our heritage were complicated. Easiest and shortest way to explain—reincarnation on my mother's part.

"I didn't mean you," Raquel replied contritely.

"Heathcliff is my thirty-fourth or seventy-eighth cousin," Astrid told her as she played with the shattered pieces of a vase that was older than dirt. "So while he may be all those other things, his line is pristine."

I had to roll my eyes at that one. I was a Vampyre and Astrid was half Vampyre and half Demon. Pristine was pushing it.

"Raquel, come with me," Astrid said as she got up and stepped on an ancient scroll. Both the bane of my existence and I winced at that one. "We'll find Samuel and you can teach him quantum physics or some other equally redonkulous bullshit like algebra."

"My pleasure," Raquel said as she waved goodbye to me with her middle finger and flounced out of the room.

That would definitely be the first body part I would remove.

"Heathcliff, you wait here. Ethan wants to talk with you."

The sound of Raquel's laughter as she sped down the hall made me grind my fangs. She wouldn't have the last laugh. Nope, I'd make sure of that.

***

"She's a pain in the ass and as difficult as they come, but she's brilliant and she's my sister. You will make this work. And for God's sake stop betting her or daring her to do things—she can't stop herself," Ethan said tersely.

My oldest and closest friend ran his hands through his hair in frustration as he took in his office. I glanced around at the disaster and looked down at the floor. I never lost control. Ever. That woman was knocking me off my game and I didn't like it.

"She not difficult. She's a fucking menace," I told him. There simply had to be another way.

"Correct." Ethan grinned, enjoying my pain. He was just as bad as his mate, Astrid. "You two are it. Astrid and I trust you with the life of our son and that is not something we do lightly."

"She blushes," I said.

"I'm sorry, what?"

"Raquel blushes," I repeated.

Ethan busied himself with trying to piece together a statue that had been the victim of Raquel's wrath. He ignored my

143

query.

"It's not normal," I went on.

"Nothing about my sister is normal. Nothing about her is typical and most of what I know about her defies logic. However, that's her story to tell. Not mine. Furthermore, you are both related by blood to my son and unfortunately the two of you are the most qualified to teach him what he needs to know," Ethan snapped as he tossed the statue into a wastebasket. "My child is six months old. He's the size of a four year old. He can turn people's skin all colors of the rainbow, not to mention he can conjure Trolls and Gnomes." Ethan shuddered. "He's been kidnapped by Fairies and he needs to be trained to defend himself. Not sure how much clearer you need me to make this."

"Let me teach him to fight and send her back to the rock she lives under," I shot back. "He doesn't need to know his multiplication tables to kill a Troll."

"And that is where you are wrong, my friend," Ethan said. "His mind is a wonder. We need to feed it and keep it occupied so he stops animating stuffed animals that have death wishes."

"You're joking."

"No, I'm not joking. Not even a little fucking bit," Ethan ground out. "Have you ever been attacked and almost decapitated by an army of orange and blue teddy bears?"

I was speechless.

"I thought not," Ethan said wearily. "Add to that a fire breathing purple plastic dragon and a dagger throwing headless doll. My son thinks this is funny."

"It actually is kind of funny."

The glare I received made me bite back the tasteless dragon joke that was on the tip of my tongue. Samuel was not just a Prince and the child of Astrid and Ethan. He was a True Immortal—one of nine. God was Good. Satan was Evil. Mother Nature was Emotion, her husband, the father of Satan was Wisdom. Hayden, the Angel of Death was Death. Elijah, the Angel of Light was Life. Dixie, Satan's daughter was Balance, her half-sister Lucy was Temptation. Astrid was Compassion and Samuel was Utopia—a combination of all of them. That kid had one Hell of a row to hoe.

"I knew this would be difficult," Ethan admitted, "but it is what it is. You'll do this because I have asked you and you will do it well."

"Yes, I will. But I won't be responsible if your sister loses a few limbs."

There was no choice in the matter. I had no issue with training the child. I adored him and it was an honor to have been

144

asked. But getting along with the shrew was difficult at best and impossible at worst.

"As long as it's not her head then I'm fine with that. Just don't do it in front of my child," Ethan said. "Clear?"

"Clear."

It was a promise I didn't know if I could keep.

Visit my website at www.robynpeterman.com.

Excerpt from *Ready To Were*

SHIFT HAPPENS SERIES Book One

Book Description

I never planned on going back to Hung Island, Georgia. Ever.

I was a top notch Were agent for the secret paranormal Council and happily living in Chicago where I had everything I needed – a gym membership, season tickets to the Cubs and Dwayne – my gay, Vampyre best friend. Going back now would mean facing the reason I'd left and I'd rather chew my own paw off than deal with Hank.

Hank the Tank Wilson was the six foot three, obnoxious, egotistical, perfect-assed, best-sex-of-my-life, Werewolf who cheated on me and broke my heart. At the time, I did what any rational woman would do. I left in the middle of the night with a suitcase, big plans and enough money for a one-way bus ticket to freedom. I vowed to never return.

But here I am, trying to wrap my head around what has happened to some missing Weres without wrapping my body around Hank. I hope I don't have to eat my words and my paw.

***This novella originally appeared in the *Three Southern Beaches* collection released July of 2014. This is an extended version of that story.

Chapter 1

"You're joking."

"No, actually I'm not," my boss said and slapped the folder into my hands. "You leave tomorrow morning and I don't want to see your hairy ass till this is solved."

I looked wildly around her office for something to lob at her head. It occurred to me that might not be the best of ideas, but desperate times led to stupid measures. She could not do this to me. I'd worked too hard and I wasn't going back. Ever.

"First of all, my ass is not hairy except on a full moon and you're smoking crack if you think I'm going back to Georgia."

Angela crossed her arms over her ample chest and narrowed her eyes at me. "Am I your boss?" she asked.

"Is this a trick question?"

She huffed out an exasperated sigh and ran her hands through her spiked 'do making her look like she'd been electrocuted. "Essie, I am cognizant of how you feel about Hung Island, Georgia, but there's a disaster of major proportions on the horizon and I have no choice."

"Where are you sending Clark and Jones?" I demanded.

"New York and Miami."

"Oh my god," I shrieked. "Who did I screw over in a former life that those douches get to go to cool cities and I have to go home to an island called Hung?"

"Those douches *do* have hairy asses and not just on a full moon. You're the only female agent I have that looks like a model so you're going to Georgia. Period."

"Fine. I'll quit. I'll open a bakery."

Angela smiled and an icky feeling skittered down my spine. "Excellent, I'll let you tell the Council that all the money they invested in your training is going to be flushed down the toilet because you want to bake cookies."

The Council consisted of supernaturals from all sorts of species. The branch that currently had me by the metaphorical balls was WTF—Werewolf Treaty Federation. They were the worst as far as stringent rules and consequences went. The Vampyres were loosey goosey, the Witches were nuts and the freakin' Fairies were downright pushovers, but not the Weres. Nope, if you enlisted you were in for life. It had sounded so good when the insanely sexy recruiting officer had come to our local Care For Your Inner Were meeting.

Training with the best of the best. Great salary with benefits. Apartment and company car. But the kicker for me was that it was fifteen hours away from the hell I grew up in. No longer was I Essie from Hung Island, Georgia—*and who in their right mind would name an island Hung*—I was Agent Essie McGee of the Chicago WTF. The irony of the initials was a source of pain to most Werewolves, but went right over the Council's heads due to the simple fact that they were older than dirt and oblivious to pop culture.

Yes, I'd been disciplined occasionally for mouthing off to superiors and using the company credit card for shoes, but other than that I was a damn good agent. I'd graduated at the top of my class and was the go-to girl for messy and dangerous assignments that no one in their right mind would take... I'd singlehandedly brought down three rogue Weres who were selling secrets to the Dragons—another supernatural species. The Dragons shunned the Council, had their own little club and a psychotic desire to rule the world. Several times they'd come close due to the fact that they were loaded and Weres from the New Jersey Pack were easily bribed. Not to mention the fire-breathing thing...

I was an independent woman living in the Windy City. I had a gym membership, season tickets to the Cubs and a gay Vampyre best friend named Dwayne. What more did a girl need?

Well, possibly sex, but the *bastard* had ruined me for other men...

Hank "The Tank" Wilson was the main reason I'd rather chew my own paw off than go back to Hung Island, Georgia. Six foot three of obnoxious, egotistical, perfect-assed, alpha male Werewolf. As the alpha of my local Pack he had decided it was high time I got mated...to him. I, on the other hand, had plans—

big ones and they didn't include being barefoot and pregnant at the beck and call of a player.

So I did what any sane, rational woman would do. I left in the middle of the night with a suitcase, a flyer from the hot recruiter and enough money for a one-way bus ticket to freedom. Of course, nothing ever turns out as planned... The apartment was the size of a shoe box, the car was used and smelled like French fries and the benefits didn't kick in till I turned one hundred and twenty five. We Werewolves had long lives.

"Angela, you really can't do this to me." Should I get down on my knees? I was so desperate I wasn't above begging.

"Why? What happened there, Essie? Were you in some kind of trouble I should know about?" Her eyes narrowed, but she wasn't yelling.

I think she liked me...kind of. The way a mother would like an annoying spastic two year old who belonged to someone else.

"No, not exactly," I hedged. "It's just that..."

"Weres are disappearing and presumed dead. Considering no one knows of our existence besides other supernaturals, we have a problem. Furthermore, it seems like humans might be involved."

My stomach lurched and I grabbed Angela's office chair for balance. "Locals are missing?" I choked out. My grandma Bobby Sue was still there, but I'd heard from her last night. She'd harangued me about getting my belly button pierced. Why I'd put that on Instagram was beyond me. I was gonna hear about that one for the next eighty years or so.

"Not just missing—more than likely dead. Check the folder," Angela said and poured me a shot of whiskey.

With trembling hands I opened the folder. This had to be a joke. I felt ill. I'd gone to high school with Frankie Mac and Jenny Packer. Jenny was as cute as a button and was the cashier at the Piggly Wiggly. Frankie Mac had been the head cheerleader and cheated on every test since the fourth grade. Oh my god, Debbie Swink? Debbie Swink had been voted most likely to succeed and could do a double backwards flip off the high dive. She'd busted her head open countless times before she'd perfected it. Her mom was sure she'd go to the Olympics.

"I know these girls," I whispered.

"Knew. You knew them. They all were taking classes at the modeling agency."

"What modeling agency? There's no modeling agency on Hung Island." I sifted through the rest of the folder with a knot the size of a cantaloupe in my stomach. More names and faces I

151

recognized. Sandy Moongie? *Wait a minute.*

"Um, not to speak ill of the dead, but Sandy Moongie was the size of a barn...she was modeling?"

"Worked the reception desk." Angela shook her head and dropped down on the couch.

"This doesn't seem that complicated. It's fairly black and white. Whoever is running the modeling agency is the perp."

"The modeling agency is Council sponsored."

I digested that nugget in silence for a moment.

"And the Council is running a modeling agency, why?"

"Word is that we're heading toward revealing ourselves to the humans and they're trying to find the most attractive representatives to do so."

"That's a joke, right?" *What kind of dumb ass plan was that?*

"I wish it was." Angela picked up my drink and downed it. "I'm getting too old for this shit," she muttered as she refilled the shot glass, thought better of it and just swigged from the bottle.

"Is the Council aware that I'm going in?"

"What do you think?"

"I think they're old and stupid and that they send in dispensable agents like me to clean up their shitshows," I grumbled.

"Smart girl."

"Who else knows about this? Clark? Jones?"

"They know," she said wearily. "They're checking out agencies in New York and Miami."

"Isn't it conflict of interest to send me where I know everyone?"

"It is, but you'll be able to infiltrate and get in faster that way. Besides, no one has disappeared from the other agencies yet."

There was one piece I still didn't understand. "How are humans involved?"

She sighed and her head dropped back onto her broad shoulders. "Humans are running the agency."

It took a lot to render me silent, like learning my grandma had been a stripper in her youth, and that all male Werewolves were hung like horses... but this was horrific.

"Who in the hell thought that was a good idea? My god, half the female Weres I know sprout tails when flash bulbs go off. We won't have to come out, they can just run billboards of hot girls with hairy appendages coming out of their asses."

"It's all part of the *Grand Plan.* If the humans see how wonderful and attractive we are, the issue of knowingly living alongside of us will be moot."

Again. Speechless.

"When are Council elections?" It was time to vote some of those turd knockers out.

"Essie." Angela rolled her eyes and took another swig. "There are no elections. They're appointed and serve for life."

"I knew that," I mumbled. Skipping Were History class was coming back to bite me in the butt.

"I'll go." There was no way I couldn't. Even though my knowledge of the hierarchy of my race was fuzzy, my skills were top notch and trouble seemed to find me. In any other job that would suck, but in mine, it was an asset.

"Good. You'll be working with the local Pack alpha. He's also the sheriff there. Name's Hank Wilson. You know him?"

"Yep." *Biblically. I knew the son of a bitch biblically.*

***

"You're gonna bang him."

"I am not gonna bang him."

"You are so gonna bang him."

"Dwayne, if I hear you say that I'm gonna bang him one more time, I will not let you borrow my black Mary Jane pumps. Ever again."

Dwayne made the international "zip the lip and throw away the key" sign while silently mouthing that I was going to bang Hank.

"I think you should bang him if he's a hot as you said." Dwayne made himself comfortable on my couch and turned on the TV.

"When did I ever say he was hot?" I demanded as I took the remote out of his hands. I was not watching any more *Dance Moms*. "I never said he was hot."

"Paaaaleese," Dwayne flicked his pale hand over his shoulder and rolled his eyes.

"What was that?"

"What was what?" he asked, confused.

"That shoulder thing you just did."

"Oh, I was flicking my hair over my shoulder in a *girlfriend* move."

"Okay, don't do that. It doesn't work. You're as bald as a cue ball."

"But it's the new move," he whined.

Oh my god, Vampyres were such high maintenance. "According to who?" I yanked my suitcase out from under my bed and started throwing stuff in.

"Kim Kardashian."

I refused to dignify that with so much as a look.

"Fine," he huffed. "But if you say one word about my skinny jeans I am so out of here."

I considered it, but I knew he was serious. As crazy as he drove me, I adored him. He was my only real friend in Chicago and I had no intention of losing him.

"I know he's hot," Dwayne said. "Look at you—you're so gorge it's redonkulous. You're all legs and boobs and hair and lips—you're far too beautiful to be hung up on a goober."

"Are you calling me shallow?" I snapped as I ransacked my tiny apartment for clean clothes. Damn it, tomorrow was laundry day. I was going to have to pack dirty clothes.

"So he's ugly and puny and wears bikini panties?"

"No! He's hotter than Satan's underpants and he wears boxer briefs," I shouted. "You happy?"

"He's actually a nice guy."

"You've met Hank?" I was so confused I was this close to making fun of his skinny jeans just so he would leave.

"Satan. He's not as bad as everyone thinks."

How was it that everyone I came in contact with today stole my ability to speak? Thankfully, I was interrupted by a knock at my door.

"You expecting someone?" Dwayne asked as he pilfered the remote back and found *Dance Moms*.

"No."

I peeked through the peephole. Nobody came to my place except Dwayne and the occasional pizza delivery guy or Chinese food take out guy or Indian food take out guy. *Wait. What the hell was my boss doing here?*

"Angela?"

"You going to let me in?"

"Depends."

"Open the damn door."

I did.

Angela tromped into my shoebox and made herself at home. Her hair was truly spectacular. It looked like she might have even pulled out a clump on the left side. "You want to tell me why the sheriff and alpha of Hung Island, Georgia says he won't work with you?"

"Um…no?"

"He said he had a hard time believing someone as flaky and irresponsible as you had become an agent for the Council and he wants someone else." Angela narrowed her eyes at me and took the remote form Dwayne. "Spill it, Essie."

I figured the best way to handle this was to lie—hugely. However, gay Vampyre boyfriends had a way of interrupting and screwing up all your plans.

"Well, you see..."

"He's her mate and he dipped his stick in several other...actually *many* other oil tanks. So she dumped his furry player ass, snuck away in the middle of the night and hadn't really planned on ever going back there again." Dwayne sucked in a huge breath, which was ridiculous because Vampyres didn't breathe.

It took everything I had not to scream and go all Wolfy. "Dwayne, clearly you want me to go medieval on your lily white ass because I can't imagine why you would utter such bullshit to my boss."

"Doesn't sound like bullshit to me," Angela said as she channel surfed and landed happily on an old episode of *Cagney and Lacey*. "We might have a problem here."

"Are you replacing me?" Hank Wilson had screwed me over once when I was his. He was not going to do it again when I wasn't.

"Your call," she said. Dwayne, who was an outstanding shoplifter, covertly took back the remote and flipped over to the Food Channel. Angela glanced up at the tube and gave Dwayne the evil eye.

"I refuse to watch lesbians fight crime in the eighties. I'll get hives," he explained, tilted his head to the right and gave Angela a smile. He was so pretty it was silly—piercing blue eyes and body to die for. Even my boss had a hard time resisting his charm.

"Fine," she grumbled.

"Excuse me," I yelled. "This conversation is about me, not testosterone ridden women cops with bad hair, hives or food. It's my life we're talking about here—me, me, me!" My voice had risen to decibels meant to attract stray animals within a ten-mile radius, evidenced by the wincing and ear covering.

"Essie, are you done?" Dwayne asked fearfully.

"Possibly. What did you tell him?" I asked Angela.

"I told him the Council has the last word in all matters. Always. And if he had a problem with it, he could take it up with the elders next month when they stay awake long enough to listen to the petitions of their people."

"Oh my god, that's awesome," I squealed. "What did he say?"

"That if we send you down, he'll give you bus money so you can hightail your sorry cowardly butt right back out of

155

town."

Was she grinning at me, and was that little shit Dwayne jotting the conversation down in the notes section on his phone?

"Let me tell you something," I ground out between clenched teeth as I confiscated Dwayne's phone and pocketed it. "I am going to Hung Island, Georgia tomorrow and I will kick his ass. I will find the killer first and then I will castrate the alpha of the Georgia Pack...with a dull butter knife."

Angela laughed and Dwayne jackknifed over on the couch in a visceral reaction to my plan. I stomped into my bathroom and slammed the door to make my point, then pressed my ear to the rickety wood to hear them talk behind my back.

"I'll bet you five hundred dollars she's gonna bang him," Dwayne told Angela.

"I'll bet you a thousand that you're right," she shot back.

"You're on."

Chapter 2

"This music is going to make me yack." Dwayne moaned and put his hands over his ears.

Trying to ignore him wasn't working. I promised myself I wouldn't put him out of the car until we were at least a hundred miles outside of Chicago. I figured anything less than that wouldn't be the kind of walk home that would teach him a lesson.

"First of all, Vampyres can't yack and I don't recall asking you to come with me," I replied and cranked up The Clash.

"You have got to be kidding." He huffed and flipped the station to Top Forty. "You need me."

"Really?"

"Oh my god," Dwayne shrieked. "I luurrve Lady Gaga."

"That's why I need you?"

"Wait. What?"

"I need you because you love The Gaga?"

Dwayne rolled his eyes. "Everyone loves The Gaga. You need me because you need to show your hometown and Hank the Hooker that you have a new man in your life."

"You're a Vampyre."

"Yes, and?"

"Well, um...you're gay."

"What does that have to do with anything? I am hotter than asphalt in August and I have a huge package."

While his points were accurate, there was no mistaking his sexual preference. The skinny jeans, starched muscle shirt, canvas Mary Janes and the gold hoop earrings were an undead giveaway.

"You know, I think you should just be my best friend. I want to show them I don't need a man to make it in this world...okay?" I glanced over and he was crying. Shitshitshit. Why did I always say the wrong thing? "Dwayne, I'm sorry. You can totally be my..."

"You really consider me your best friend?" he blubbered. "I have never had a best friend in all my three hundred years. I've tried, but I just..." He broke down and let her rip.

"Yes, you're my best friend, you idiot. Stop crying. Now." Snark I could deal with. Tears? Not so much.

"Oh my god, I just feel so happy," he gushed. "And I want you to know if you change your mind about the boyfriend thing just wink at me four times and I'll stick my tongue down your throat."

"Thanks, I'll keep that in mind."

"Anything for my best friend. Ohhh Essie, are there any gay bars in Hung?"

This was going to be a wonderful trip.

***

One way in to Hung Island, Georgia. One way out. The bridge was long and the ocean was beautiful. Sun glistened off the water and sparkled like diamonds. Dwayne was quiet for the first time in fifteen hours. As we pulled into town, my gut clenched and I started to sweat. This was stupid—so very stupid. The nostalgic pull of this place was huge and I felt sucked back in immediately.

"Holy Hell," Dwayne whispered. "It's beautiful here. How did you leave this place?"

He was right. It was beautiful. It had the small town feel mixed up with the ocean and land full of wild grasses and rolling hills. How did I leave?

"I left because I hate it here," I lied. "We'll do the job, castrate the alpha with a butter knife and get out. You got it?"

"Whatever you say, best friend. Whatever you say." He grinned.

"I'm gonna drop you off at my Grandma Bobby Sue's. She doesn't exactly know we're coming so you have to be on your best behavior."

"Will you be?"

"Will I be what?" God, Vamps were tiresome.

"On your best behavior."

"Absolutely not. We're here."

I stopped my crappy car in front of a charming old

158

Craftsman. Flowers covered every inch of the yard. It was a literal explosion of riotous color and I loved it. Granny hated grass—found the color offensive. It was the home I grew up in. Granny BS, as everyone loved to call her, had raised me after my parents died in a horrific car accident when I was four. I barely remembered my parents, but Granny had told me beautiful bedtime stories about them my entire childhood.

"OMG, this place is so cute I could scream." Dwayne squealed and jumped out of the car into the blazing sunlight. All the stories about Vamps burning to ash or sparkling like diamonds in the sun were a myth. The only thing that could kill Weres and Vamps were silver bullets, decapitation, fire and a silver stake in the heart.

Grabbing Dwayne by the neck of his muscle shirt, I stopped him before he went tearing into the house. "Granny is old school. She thinks Vamps are...you know."

"Blood sucking leeches who should be eliminated?" Dwayne grinned from ear to ear. He loved a challenge. Crap.

"I wouldn't go that far, but she's old and set in her geezer ways. So if you have to, steer clear."

"I'll have her eating kibble out of my manicured lily white hand in no time at...holy shit!" Dwayne screamed and ducked as a blur of Granny BS came flying out of the house and tackled my ass in a bed of posies.

"Mother Humper." I grunted and struggled as I tried to shove all ninety-five pounds of pissed off Grandma Werewolf away from me.

"Gimme that stomach," she hissed as she yanked up my shirt. Thank the Lord I was wearing a bra. Dwayne stood in mute shock and just watched me get my butt handed to me by my tiny granny, who even at eighty was the spitting image of a miniature Sophia Loren in her younger years.

"Get off of me, you crazy old bag," I ground out and tried to nail her with a solid left. She ducked and backslapped my head.

"I said no tattoos and no piercings till you're fifty," she yelled. "Where is it?"

"Oh my GOD," I screeched as I trapped her head with my legs in a scissors hold. "You need meds."

"Tried 'em. They didn't work," she grumbled as she escaped from my hold. She grabbed me from behind as I tried to make a run for my car and ripped out my belly button ring.

"Ahhhhhhgrhupcraaap, that hurt, you nasty old bat from Hell." I screamed and looked down at the bloody hole that used to be really cute and sparkly. "That was a one carat diamond, you ancient witch."

Both of her eyebrows shot up and I swear to god they touched her hairline.

"Okay, fine," I muttered. "It was cubic zirconia, but it was NOT cheap."

"Hookers have belly rings," she snapped.

"No, hookers have pimps. Normal people have belly rings, or at least they used to," I shot back as I examined the wound that was already closing up.

"Come give your granny a hug," she said and put her arms out.

I approached warily just in case she needed to dole out more punishment for my piercing transgression. She folded me into her arms and hugged me hard. That was the thing about my granny. What you saw was what you got. Everyone always knew where they stood with her. She was mad and then she was done. Period.

"Lawdy, I have missed you, child," she cooed.

"Missed you too, you old cow." I grinned and hugged her back. I caught Dwayne out of the corner of my eye. He was even paler than normal if that was possible and he had placed his hands over his pierced ears.

"Granny, I brought my..."

"Gay Vampyre best friend," she finished my introduction. She marched over to him, slapped her hands on her skinny hips and stared. She was easily a foot shorter than Dwayne, but he trembled like a baby. "Do you knit?" she asked him.

"Um...no, but I've always wanted to learn," he choked out.

She looked him up and down for a loooong minute, grunted and nodded her head. "We'll get along just fine then. Get your asses inside before the neighbors call the cops."

"Why would they call the cops?" Dwayne asked, still terrified.

"Well boy, I live amongst humans and I just walloped my granddaughter on the front lawn. Most people don't think that's exactly normal."

"Point," he agreed and hightailed it to the house.

"Besides," she cackled. "Wouldn't want the sheriff coming over to arrest you now, would we?"

I rolled my eyes and flipped her the bird behind her back.

"Saw that, girlie," she said.

Holy Hell, she still had eyes in the back of her head. If I was smart, I'd grab Dwayne, get in my car and head back to Chicago...but I had a killer to catch and a whole lot to prove here. Smart wasn't on my agenda today.

Chapter 3

The house was exactly the same as it was the last time I saw it a year ago. Granny had more crap on her tables, walls and shelves than an antique store. Dwayne was positively speechless and that was good. Granny took her décor seriously.

"I'm a little disappointed that you want to be a model, Essie," Granny sighed. "You have brains and a mean right hook. Never thought you'd try to coast by with your looks."

I gave Dwayne the *I'll kill you if you tell her I'm an agent on a mission* look and thankfully he understood. While I hated that my granny thought I was shallow and jobless, it was far safer that she didn't know why I was really here.

"Well, you know...I just need to make a few bucks, then get back to my life in the big city," I mumbled. I was a sucky liar around my granny and she knew it.

"Hmmm," she said, staring daggers at me.

"What?" I asked, not exactly making eye contact.

"Nothin'. I'm just lookin'," she challenged.

"And what are you looking at?" I blew out an exasperated sigh and met her eyes. A challenge was a challenge and I *was* a Werewolf...

"A bald face little fibber girl," she crowed. "Spill it or I'll whoop your butt again."

Dwayne quickly backed himself into a corner and slid his phone out of his pocket. That shit was going to video my ass kicking. I had several choices here...destroy Dwayne's phone, elaborate on my lie or come clean. The only good option was the phone.

"Fine," I snapped and sucked in a huge breath. The truth will set you free or result in a trip to the ER... "I'm an agent with the Council—a trained killer for WTF and I'm good at it. The fact that I'm a magnet for trouble has finally paid off. I'm down here to find out who in the hell is killing Werewolves before it blows up in our faces. I plan to find the perps and destroy them with my own hands or a gun, whichever will be most painful. Then I'm going to castrate Hank with a dull butter knife. I plan on a short vacation when I'm done before going back to Chicago."

For the first time in my twenty-eight years on Earth, Granny was mute. It was all kinds of awesome.

"Can I come on the vacation?" Dwayne asked.

"Yes. Cat got your tongue, old woman?" I asked.

"Well, I'll be damned," she said almost inaudibly. "I suppose this shouldn't surprise me. You are a female alpha bitch."

"No," I corrected her. "I'm a lone wolf who wants nothing to do with Pack politics. Ever."

Granny sat her skinny bottom down on her plastic slipcovered floral couch and shook her head. "Ever is a long time, little girl. Well, I suppose I should tell you something now," she said gravely and worried her bottom lip.

"Oh my god, are you sick?" I gasped. Introspective thought was way out of my granny's normal behavior pattern. My stomach roiled. She was all I had left in the world and as much as I wanted to skin her alive, I loved her even more.

"Weres don't get sick. It's about your mamma and daddy. Sit down. And Dwayne, hand over your phone. If I find out you have loose lips, I'll remove them," she told my bestie.

I sat. Dwayne handed. I had thought I knew everything there was to know about my parents, but clearly I was mistaken. Hugely mistaken.

"You remember when I told you your mamma and daddy died in a car accident?"

"Yes," I replied slowly. "You showed me the newspaper articles."

"That's right." She nodded. "They did die in a car, but it wasn't no accident."

Movement was necessary or I thought I might throw up. I paced the room and tried to untangle my thoughts. It wasn't like I'd even known my parents, but they were mine and now I felt cheated somehow. I wanted to crawl out of my skin. My heart pounded so loudly in my chest I was sure the neighbors could hear it. My parents were murdered and this was the first time I was hearing about it?

"Again. Say that again." Surely I'd misunderstood. I'd always been one to jump to conclusions my entire life, but the look on Granny's face told me that this wasn't one of those times.

"They didn't own a hardware store. Well, actually I think they did, but it was just a cover."

"For what?" I asked, fairly sure I knew where this was going.

"They were WTF agents, child, and they were taken out," she said and wrapped her skinny little arms around herself. "Broke my heart—still does."

"And you never told me this? Why?" I demanded and got right up in her face.

"I don't rightly know," she said quietly. "I wanted you to grow up happy and not feel the need for revenge."

She stroked my cheek the way she did when I was a child and I leaned into her hand for comfort. I was angry, but she did what she thought was right. Needless to say, she wasn't right, but…

"Wait, why would I have felt the need for revenge?" I asked. Something was missing.

"The Council was never able to find out who did it, and after a while they gave up."

Everything about that statement was so wrong I didn't know how to react. They gave up? What the hell was that? The Council never gave up. I was trained to get to the bottom of everything. Always.

"That's the most absurd thing I've ever heard. The Council always gets their answers."

Granny shrugged her thin shoulders and rearranged the knickknacks on her coffee table. Wait. Did the Council know more about me than I did? Did my boss Angela know more of my history than I'd ever known?

"I knew that recruiter they sent down here," Granny muttered. "I told him to stay away from you. Told him the Council already took my daughter and son-in-law and they couldn't have you."

"He didn't pay me any more attention than he did anyone else," I told her.

"What did the flyer say that he gave you?"

"Same as everybody's—salary, training, benefits, car, apartment."

"Damn it to hell," she shouted. "No one else's flyer said that. I confiscated them all after the bastard left. I couldn't get to yours cause you were shacking up with the sheriff."

"You lived with Hank the Hooker?" Dwayne gasped. "I thought you just dated a little."

"Hell to the no," Granny corrected Dwayne. "She was engaged. Left the alpha of the Georgia Pack high and dry."

"Enough," I snapped. "Ancient history. I'm more concerned about what kind of cow patty I've stepped in with the Council. The *sheriff* knows why I left. Maybe the Council accepted me cause I can shoot stuff and I have no fear and they have to hire a certain quota of women and..."

"And they want to make sure you don't dig into the past," Dwayne added unhelpfully.

"You're a smart bloodsucker," Granny chimed in.

"Thank you."

"You think the Council had something to do with it," I said. This screwed with my chi almost as much as the Hank situation from a year ago. I had finally done something on my own and it might turn out I hadn't earned any of it.

"I'm not sayin' nothing like that," Granny admonished harshly. "And neither should you. You could get killed."

She was partially correct, but I was the one they sent to kill people who broke Council laws. However, speaking against the Council wasn't breaking the law. The living room had grown too small for my need to move and I prowled the rest of the house with Granny and Dwayne on my heels. I stopped short and gaped at my empty bedroom.

"Where in the hell is my furniture?"

"You moved all your stuff to Hank's and he won't give it back," Granny informed me.

An intense thrill shot through my body, but I tamped it down immediately. I was done with him and he was surely done with me. No one humiliated an alpha and got a second chance. Besides, I didn't want one... Dwayne's snicker earned him a glare that made him hide behind Granny in fear.

"Did you even try to get my stuff back?" I demanded.

"Of course I did," she huffed. "That was your mamma's set from when she was a child. I expected you'd use it for your own daughter someday."

My mamma...My beautiful mamma who'd been murdered along with my daddy. The possibility that the Council had been involved was gnawing at my insides in a bad way.

"I have to compartmentalize this for a minute or at least a couple of weeks," I said as I stood in the middle of my empty bedroom. "I have to do what I was sent here for. But when I'm done, I'll get answers and vengeance."

"Does that mean no vacation?" Dwayne asked.

164

I stared at Dwayne like he'd grown three heads. He was getting terribly good at rendering me mute.

"That was a good question, Dwayne." Granny patted him on the head like a dog and he preened. "Essie, your mamma and daddy would want you to have a vacation before you get killed finding out what happened to them."

"Can we go to Jamaica?" Dwayne asked.

"Ohhh, I've never been to Jamaica," Granny volunteered.

They were both batshit crazy, but Jamaica did sound kind of nice...

"Fine, but you're paying," I told Dwayne. He was richer than Midas. He'd made outstanding investments in his three hundred years.

"Yayayayayayay!" he squealed.

"I'll call the travel agent," Granny said. "How long do you need to get the bad guy?"

"A week. Give me a week."

** Visit www.robynpeterman.com for more information.**

Book Lists (in correct reading order)

HOT DAMNED SERIES
Fashionably Dead
Fashionably Dead Down Under
Hell on Heels
Fashionably Dead in Diapers
Fashionably Hotter Than Hell

SHIFT HAPPENS SERIES
Ready to Were
Some Were in Time

MAGIC AND MAYHEM SERIES
Switching Hour
Witch Glitch

HANDCUFFS AND HAPPILY EVER AFTERS SERIES
How Hard Can it Be?
Size Matters
Cop a Feel

If after reading all the above you are still wanting more adventure and zany fun, read *Pirate Dave and His Randy Adventures*, the romance novel budding novelist Rena was helping wicked Evangeline write in *How Hard Can It Be?*

Warning: Pirate Dave Contains Romance Satire, Spoofing, and Pirates with Two Pork Swords.

About the Author

Robyn Peterman writes because the people inside her head won't leave her alone until she gives them life on paper.

Her addictions include laughing really hard with friends, shoes (the expensive kind), Target, Coke Zero Cherry with extra ice in a styrofoam cup, bejeweled reading glasses, her kids, her super-hot hubby and collecting stray animals.

A former professional actress, with Broadway, film and T.V. credits, she now lives in the south with her family and too many animals to count.

Writing gives her peace and makes her whole, plus having a job where you can work in your underpants works really well for her. You can leave Robyn a message via the Contact Page and she'll get back to you as soon as her bizarre life permits! She loves to hear from her fans!

Made in the USA
Columbia, SC
16 June 2017